For Mariana, John and Simon,
with love

G'day Mate!
This story takes place in Australia — so if you want to brush up on your Aussie slang (what are "brumbies"?), just flip to the helpful glossary at the back of the book!

One

Horse, Sweet Horse

'I am so glad to see you!' My best friend Becky Cho cantered down our driveway and flew from the saddle in a mad flurry of arms, legs and long black plaits. Her amazing bay Welsh-Arab gelding, Charlie, gazed at his mistress for a moment with adoring brown eyes then dropped his head and tore at a patch of lush green grass, his silver bit jangling as he chewed.

I wrapped my arms around Becky's neck and squealed with joy. I had just spent four weeks at Waratah Grove Riding Academy, the most awesome riding school in the country. It had been the toughest but most amazing time of my horsy life and I'd made two incredible new friends, Tash

Symon and Molly Bryant. But I was totally stoked to be back home in Shady Creek. After all, it's not easy living without one of your two best friends in the whole entire world. I guess I'd kind of missed Mum and Dad as well.

'I wanted to come straight over and see you last night but Mum said I had to rest.' I gave Becky a stern Mum-ish face and wagged my finger at her then pulled her into another tight hug. 'I missed you so much!'

Becky coughed loudly in my ear and gasped. 'You're choking me!'

I released her, looped my lead rope over my shoulder and clapped my hands. 'Today is going to be so cool. Our first Riding Club meeting together in ages.'

'So how was it, Waratah Grove?' Becky gushed. 'I want every single detail.'

'Awesome,' I sighed. 'It was so unreal, but so totally hard.'

I told her everything. About riding against the best junior riders anywhere and having to prove I had what it took to graduate. I told her about Brooke Barnes and Juliette, the dreaded Iced Vovos, and how they pretended to be my friends then turned most of my cabin against me.

Becky's eyes grew wider and wider. 'Sounds horrible. Glad it was you and not me.'

'Funny,' I said. 'But that was nothing compared to what happened with Honey.'

I told her about Honey's fear of the dressage arena and the abuse she'd suffered at the hands of her former rider.

'That's sick,' Becky said, shaking her head.

'But we got through it,' I said. 'Together. She faced her fear and came through it. We passed, Beck. We made the Honour Board.'

Becky hugged me. 'That's brilliant!'

I nodded, so glad to be with her again I could barely speak. We broke apart.

Becky slapped Charlie's neck affectionately and scratched gently behind his ears. His head drooped instantly. 'How's your mum? When's she having the baby?'

'Soon. I hope it's a girl.'

'Are you nuts?' Becky's eyes were wide with disbelief.

I giggled. 'Maybe, but I've always wanted a sister.'

'Sisters are totally overrated.' Becky's big sister, Rachael, was the world's worst sister advertisement. She was always on the phone, hogging the computer or locking Becky out of the bathroom. And worst of all, she'd given up riding and completely ignored her sweet Appaloosa mare, Cassata. I adore Cassata. She'd just spent the summer with me and Jenna, my best friend from the city, who'd learned to ride on her. I missed Jenna so much, especially now that she was in Italy with her mum and I couldn't call her. We'd been emailing each other at least once a week, but it wasn't the same. You can't be best friends with someone since kindy and not miss them like crazy!

'What else is happening? I feel like I've been gone for years.'

Becky shrugged, tying Charlie's reins to a loop of twine. She ticked her list off on her fingers. 'Dad has a special announcement to make at Riding Club today. Rachael is being her usual pain-in-the-saddle self and the Creepketeers have been up to their old tricks.'

My heart smashed into my ribcage. The Creepketeers, Carly Barnes, Flea Fowler and Ryan Thomas, have two aims in life — making my and

Becky's lives as miserable as possible and taking being utter creeps to new and unexplored levels. They hate us and we hate them. It's perfect.

'What've they been up to?'

Becky rolled her eyes. 'Have you forgotten they're in our class this year? I've had them all to myself for the past four weeks!'

I moaned, slapping my forehead with my hand. I had almost forgotten, what with the Iced Vovos to contend with and Honey's trauma and making new friends and the Waratah Grove Honour Board. I felt my body thump back to earth, hard.

'Isn't it bad enough I have to live next door to Flea? Don't we suffer enough at Riding Club?' I kicked an almost perfectly round ball of horse poo down the driveway.

'Apparently not,' Becky muttered. 'But look on the bright side.'

I glowered. The morning was sunny and warm, although it was early May. But Becky's news was enough to make me feel like I was standing in a snowstorm in my birthday suit. 'What bright side?'

Becky's eyes sparkled. 'We'll always have each other.'

'Best friends?' I held out my hand.

Becky squeezed it. 'Besties forever.' We shook on it.

'There's some other news,' Becky said, casually pulling up a long blade of grass and wedging it between her teeth. 'A new riding school is opening up in a month or so.'

She had a strange, pinched look on her face. A look I hadn't seen since the summer. But I was bursting. A new riding school in Shady Creek was just what we needed.

'I know, I can't wait!'

'Whaddya mean you know?' Becky's eyes widened. The grass fell from her lips.

'Mum told me on the way home.'

'Whaddya mean you can't wait?' I was sensing she didn't share my enthusiasm.

'Mum got me a job there,' I said. 'She met the owner somewhere and they need riders.'

Becky folded her arms, frowning so deeply she could have held twenty cent pieces in the creases in her brow.

I nudged her gently. 'C'mon, Beck. This is our first day together in forever. Anyway, what's the problem?'

Becky shook her head and the frown disappeared. 'Nothing.'

'Great!' It was so good to be with her again. 'Besides, we should celebrate the fact that Honey's horrible old owners have sold up and they'll never ever come back and finally something good for horsekind is being done on that place. Sort of makes up for what Honey went through.'

I opened the gate to Honey's paddock. My gorgeous chestnut mare looked up from where she was grazing and whinnied. My heart swelled. I hadn't known it was possible to love anyone so much.

'Honey!' I called, pulling a slice of carrot out of the waistband of my joddies. She nodded her sweet head and walked towards me, her nostrils flaring.

She nuzzled my hand for her treat. I clipped my lead rope to her halter as she crunched and slipped my arms around her firm neck, breathing in her warm, horsy smell and rubbing my fingers in her mane. I loved moments like this. It was like there was nothing and no one else in the whole world but Honey and me.

Becky cleared her throat. 'Ash, I know it's only down the street, but we're due at Riding Club in precisely—' She peered at her watch. 'Eight minutes.'

It was Sunday, and a Riding Club day. Honey was saddled in two minutes and bridled in one. After a quick stretch of her legs to make sure the girth couldn't pinch her skin, I mounted, settling into the saddle and gathering my reins. I grinned at Becky. I was home.

Two

Game for Anything

'Inspection!' boomed a familiar voice as Becky and I made a horseback beeline for the long straight row of mounted Shady Creek riders. Gary Cho, our totally amazing instructor (and Becky's very horsy dad), pushed back his tatty blue Shady Creek Riding Club cap so high I could actually see his eyes. 'Ashleigh Miller! Great to have you back.'

'Hi, Gary.' I grinned, parking Honey in the Under 12s section. Unfortunately, parking in the Under 12s section means parking next to the Creepketeers. Thankfully there are a few friendlier faces. Julie and Jodie, the identical twin Under 10s bounced in their saddles and waved frantically. And

Destiny, Carly's beautiful white mare, greeted Honey with a gentle touch, nostril to nostril.

'Everyone say "Welcome back" to Ashleigh.' Gary swelled. He was as proud as a new foal's father that one of his riders had made it to Waratah Grove. Mum had told me that he'd asked to have me dipped in bronze and mounted on the roof of his dilapidated office.

'Wel-come back, Ash-leigh,' the riders yelled, school singsong style. Carly pretended to vomit into an imaginary bucket, Flea burped along in time and Ryan dug around in his left ear with his thick forefinger then stared at its contents. Becky and the twins gave me a round of applause.

'Ash made all of us proud at Waratah Grove,' Gary said, beaming up at me. I shrank into my saddle. 'We couldn't have asked for a better representative of Shady Creek Riding Club.'

'Thanks,' I muttered.

Carly, in true Creepketeer style, coughed so loudly I was certain she'd bring up a hairball, but Becky squeezed my hand. She knew her dad could be totally embarrassing sometimes. And besides, if she hadn't broken her arm it would have been

Becky riding for that spot at Waratah Grove and I know she'd have won. She's the best junior rider in the whole district.

Gary began his usual gear and uniform check starting with the youngest riders, the Under 10s, on his left and moving across to the seniors on his right. A few riders were scolded for their sloppy uniforms and told to dismount and tuck in their blue Riding Club shirts. A boy I'd never seen before was sent home to replace his expensive-looking joggers with regulation riding boots. Carly leaned over to check how far Gary had progressed down the line then turned to us with a smile so fake it looked like it had been painted on by a three-year-old.

'The world-famous Spiller Miller! It's sooo nice to have you back at Riding Club. Not!' Carly smirked and batted her eyelashes. I prickled all over.

'Still calling me Spiller Miller?' I'd really thought that Waratah Grove would have changed all that. One fall from Scud, Flea's horrible horse, on my first day in Shady Creek and I was stuck with my dreaded nickname forever. I clenched my jaws so tightly my gums ached. 'I hoped you would've thought something new up while I was away.'

'Spiller Miller — is that what I could smell?' Flea, the grottiest boy I've ever known with a mess of colonised-by-a-family-of-marsupials brown hair on his head, waved at the air in front of his nose. He gagged then collapsed onto Scud's neck with his eyes rolling and his tongue hanging out. Ryan guffawed, a noise that made a choking chimpanzee sound like a celestial choir. His huge grey gelding, Arnie, flicked his ears but otherwise paid no attention. Carly shrieked with ear-ringing laughter. Even the nasty pure black gelding, Scud, looked like he was enjoying the joke. I could have sworn the horse was sneering.

'Nothing's changed I see, Frederick,' I said, leaning forward to check Honey's girth by sliding my fingers under it. It was pretty roomy down there, so I moved my left leg forward and, holding onto my reins with my right hand, tightened the girth with my left hand. Honey shook her head as if to say, 'What did you do that for? The girth was much more comfortable when it was nice and loose!' I could see her point, but winding up under her belly during a Riding Club meeting wasn't exactly what I had planned for the day.

Flea's mouth dropped open. Even his rat's nest hair looked shocked. He hates being called Frederick as much as I hate the Creeps calling me Spiller Miller.

Becky nodded, her eyes narrow. 'I can tell you one thing that's changed. Ashleigh kicked serious butt at Waratah Grove. But I guess you heard all about that from your cousin, right, Carly?'

Carly's face flushed pink and her red hair, pulled back in its usual tight neat bun at the base of her skinny neck, looked like it would throw off sparks. She was obviously not too pleased that her plans to ruin my stay at the Grove through her cousin Brooke had failed as miserably as a Shetland running the Melbourne Cup (not that I wouldn't love to see that!). 'Why don't you just zip your lip, Rebecca's Garden? This has nothing—'

'Don't call me that.' Becky's pretty face was scrunched into a mask of utter contempt. She's never forgiven her parents for naming their Chinese restaurant after her.

Carly stiffened. Her eyes flashed. 'Who's gunna stop me?'

'Yeah,' said Ryan, his finger back at work inside his ear.

Gary finally reached me in the inspection line-up. 'Talk about good timing,' I muttered, torn between utter loathing for the Creeps and wanting to plant a humungous kiss on Gary's cheek before he moved on to finish inspecting the others.

'Listen up, people.' Gary clapped his hands then stood up on the dusty blue upturned milk crate he used as a platform. 'I have some exciting news for you that I know you've all been waiting for. The next Zone Gymkhana is on Saturday in just eight weeks' time—'

'Yes!' I cried.

'Good to see you're rearing to go.' Gary laughed. 'Ha. Get it?'

Becky moaned and buried her face in her gloved hands. I patted her knee. There is nothing worse in the universe for one's social, emotional and mental health than an embarrassing parent. Trust me, I know. Mum was still wearing her navy blue plumbing overalls in public, despite being a hundred and twenty-seven months pregnant.

'We'll be organising ourselves into teams today,' Gary continued. 'I also have a stack of entry forms for those of you who'll be entering individual events.' Gary peered at us, a look I knew only too well, a look that meant 'you will enter and you will win'.

It was then that it hit me like a fully loaded muck-out barrow.

'Eight weeks away,' I hissed to Becky. 'But that's—'

'My birthday,' Becky said, a smile tugging at her lips.

I beamed. 'Cool!'

'A gymkhana is all about fun,' Gary continued, 'but mounted games can also help improve your skills and, one day, may take you all the way to the top of national and international competition. So, basically you're having a great time and learning to be better equestrians while you're at it.'

'What kind of mounted games?' Sandra Jones who rode a plucky dark brown pony called Chocolate waved her hand in the air.

Gary pulled a piece of paper from the back pocket of his jeans and squinted at it. 'Potato race, bottle race, egg and spoon race and sack race.'

'Egg and spoon race!' Carly shrieked at once. 'That's so babyish! I bet there'll be no egg and spoon races at the new riding school.'

Gary's eyes flicked to Carly's face and she snapped her mouth shut.

'We'll go through the rules of each game then have a go for real. Carly, you'll go first in the egg and spoon. Then you'll see first-hand the level of skill required by a rider to compete and win in these events.'

Carly looked like she'd just been force-fed the egg, spoon and all. I sat up in the saddle, hoping that wiggling my backside would open my ears and improve my memory. Honey chomped down on her bit and tugged at the reins as if to say, 'Enough talk — let's get moving!'

'In the egg and spoon race each team gets one dessertspoon and one egg and there are three bending poles on the course.' Gary looked serious. It was like nothing mattered to him more in the world than Riding Club games. It's one of the things I love about our club. 'Rider One carries the egg and spoon, bends through the first two poles and around the third, then rides back through the poles to Rider Two. Rider One hands the egg and spoon over and Rider Two repeats the course and so on. Riders should canter, or trot at the slowest.'

'Easy,' Carly said. 'Too easy.'

'We'll see,' Gary said. He disappeared into his office for a moment and came back with a cardboard fruit box. 'This is one of the spoons we'll be practising with.'

Gary held up a metal spoon with red tape stuck around the middle.

'What's that tape for?' Jodie asked, frowning. 'Is it for grip?'

'It's a marker,' I said, defying the Creeps to call me a know-all. 'You can't hold the spoon above the tape.'

'Spot on, Ashleigh,' Gary said. 'And that's one of the things that makes this race so challenging — passing the spoon from one rider to another without crossing the red line. Another is getting around that third pole with the reins in one hand and a jiggling egg in the other.'

'What if you drop the egg?' Julie exchanged glances with her sister. I grinned. It was going to be so cool having a sister of my own. I couldn't wait. I had it all planned out. I was going to teach her everything I knew about horses and riding and—

'Good question,' Gary said, shaking me out of my daydream. 'If a rider drops the egg, he or she has to pick it up with the spoon, mounted, or dismount to do it then continue from the point where they dropped the egg. You are not to touch the egg with anything but the spoon.'

'Wow,' Becky said.

'Wow,' Carly mimicked, twisting her face into a horrible mask. I gave her the nastiest look I could manage, vowing to never ever leave Becky alone in Shady Creek again.

Gary was oblivious. 'Take my advice and don't drop your egg. It's hard for any team to recover from a mistake like that.'

'What about the other races?' Ryan called out, his finger digging in his ear again. I stared at him in wonder. Every now and then Ryan says something worth listening to. This was one of those times.

'The bottle race is like a relay race using plastic sports bottles instead of batons,' Gary explained. 'Each team has two bottles. Rider One starts with a bottle then rides to an upturned bin on the centre line and places the bottle on the bin. They ride on to the far end where there's another bin with the team's second bottle on top. The rider grabs it, gallops back to the starting line and hands it over to

Rider Two. Rider Two rides to the far bin, places the bottle on top, rides to the first bin, collects the bottle and rides back to the starting line. Riders Three and Four repeat the process. Are we all clear?'

I nodded, leaned over in my saddle and nudged Becky with my elbow. She grabbed my hand, giving it a squeeze. I couldn't wait to get started! After those four unbelievable, but sometimes very stressful, weeks at Waratah Grove some high-speed mounted games were just what I needed.

Gary had us warm-up our horses at last. Carly moaned and rolled her eyes, but I love the warm-up. It's not only necessary to prepare the horse for the work he or she is about to do (you try getting straight out of bed and galloping around a paddock carrying a kid on your back), but it's also a time to just concentrate on Honey. There's no race, no keeping score. There's just me and my horse alone together, moving as one, breathing as one, being as one. I lost myself in Honey, hearing nothing but the beating of her hooves, seeing nothing but her mane bouncing with her strides. How did people live without horses? How could people not love them? How could they go through life never having sat in a saddle or felt the warmth of a horse's shoulder against their skin or galloped so fast that for a split second they felt like they were flying? I knew I'd never figure it out.

'Ashleigh Miller!' I was jerked out of my delicious horsy daydream by Gary's voice and pulled Honey up from her figure eight.

I could hear laughter. Every single Shady Creek rider was waiting for me. Gary had been calling me, but I'd travelled so far into Horseland I hadn't heard him.

'Sorry, Gary,' I muttered, pulling up into the line again.

'Typical,' Carly whispered. 'No wonder you stank at the Grove.'

'At least I got there,' I hissed. 'Which is more than you'll ever—'

'You know yourselves how old you're turning this year so you should know which team you'll be on,' Gary said before I'd had a chance to catch up on the month's worth of anti-Creep remarks I'd been busting to make. 'So if you're an Under 10, form a team of four Under 10s. If you're an Under 12 do the same and so on.'

So that was it? He was just going to let us form our own teams?

Becky, the Creeps and I just stood there, watching the other teams sort themselves out and watching each other. There were five of us. And only four places on the team. This had happened once before when I had taken Ryan's place, making him the number five. The Creeps had made things harder for me then more than ever. No one would make the first move. No one dared.

'What's going on?' Gary appeared out of nowhere at Becky's side.

'Nothing,' she muttered.

'I can see nothing's going on. That's the problem. You guys should have figured it all out by now. It's not hard to make two teams of four.'

Becky raised her eyebrows. 'Two teams?'

Gary shrugged. 'Yeah. We've had a few birthdays.'

'Ash, Beck, wanna be on our team?' Someone behind us giggled.

I twisted around in the saddle. 'Do I ever!'

Julie and Jodie high-fived Becky and me. With their identical long dark hair, brown eyes and infectious smiles they were so alike that sometimes I

21

could only tell them apart by who was riding whom and the different coloured ribbons they wore in their hair — red for Julie, blue for Jodie. Boots, Julie's cute bay Welsh Mountain pony gelding with a look in his eye as cheeky as hers, danced on his sturdy forelegs. He was as impatient to get started as we were.

'Poor Sandra!' Becky said suddenly. Our new team looked on as Sandra and Chocolate took their place next to the Creeps. Sandra sneezed violently. Carly recoiled and brushed down her immaculate joddies.

'I wonder if she's allergic to them as well?' I mused. Sandra has more allergies than anyone I've ever known. She's often away from Riding Club because of her horsehair allergy.

Becky grabbed my arm, squeezing hard. 'Do you know what this means?'

'Ow!' I prised at her fingers.

Becky shook her head. 'It means they're on another team to us!'

Julie, Jodie and I exchanged glances. Becky sure was getting slow in her old age.

Becky groaned. 'It means we ride against them.

Wasn't it bad enough riding *with* them?' Her dark eyes were wide with the look of someone who'd just remembered something truly awful.

I shrugged. 'Yeah, but—'

'Don't you get it?' Becky's voice was shrill. 'Remember what they did to us at the last gymkhana? And that was when they were on our team.'

Jodie offered her hand. Julie did the same. Becky grabbed their hands then it was my turn. All for one and one for all.

'Now that you're in your teams we'll have a go at the first race.' Gary was standing on his blue milk crate. 'Have a good look at the course.'

On the flat, open paddock that we used for all our training, Gary had set up five lines of three bending poles placed about 7 metres apart. My heart pounded. I couldn't wait to get out there.

'The starting line is here,' Gary said, kicking at a clump of tufty bush grass that sat about 5 metres from the first pole. 'Rider One will take the egg and spoon in one hand and ride the course as fast as they can,' Gary continued. I grinned at Becky and gave her the thumbs up. She held up the egg and spoon and gave me one of her extra special smiles.

'It's best to hold the spoon as far from your body as you can and take extra care on that last pole. Have all the Rider Fours got their bands on?'

I touched my helmet with my fingertips. Yep, my white band, which would let the judges know I was Rider Four, was still there.

'On your marks.'

Becky moved into position. Julie and Jodie lined up behind her.

'Get set.'

I gathered my reins and leaned forward a little in the saddle.

'Go!'

Charlie burst from the starting line and tore down the course bending left around the first pole then right around the second. Becky kept Charlie's nose close to the third pole as they twisted around it. They cantered back through the poles and then home.

Julie held out her hand. 'Here, Becky, here!'

Becky handed the spoon over carefully, as though it were a butterfly. Julie made sure her fingers stayed below the red tape. Once she had a grip on the spoon Julie drummed her heels on Boots's sides and he leapt out onto the course.

'Go, Julie!' I screamed, sneaking a sideways glance at the Creeps. Ryan, their Rider Two, was out on the course, just a nose in front of Julie. Arnie had a distinct advantage over Boots in the length department, but Boots made up for it with sheer spunk and his strong, quick pony legs.

Boots scrambled back to the starting line, Julie holding out the spoon to her sister. Jodie made a swipe at the spoon and the egg flew over her pony's shoulder (thank goodness it was just a golf ball!).

'Get it!' Becky cried. Jodie leaned over in the saddle, scooped up the egg with the spoon and, with only the slightest nudge, burst out from the starting line on her pixie-faced black Dartmoor pony, Buttons.

'Go, Jodie!' Julie and I shrieked. I was so nervous, so excited and so scared all at once. I was out next. We'd lost time with that drop of the egg and I was riding against Carly. Everybody knows that there's nothing Carly loves more in the whole world than beating me, especially in riding. And there's nothing I hate more in the entire world than letting her do it.

Jodie and Buttons twisted neatly around the last pole, Jodie's eyes fixed on the egg as though it was a bomb about to explode.

I gathered my reins into my left hand.

Jodie bent Buttons through the second pole.

I flexed the fingers of my right hand and settled deep into the saddle, feeling Honey tense underneath me in anticipation.

Jodie cleared the first pole and cantered back to the starting line, her right hand outstretched, neck and neck with Sandra and Chocolate.

'You can do it,' I told myself. 'Honey can do it.'

I held out my hand. Jodie offered me the spoon. I took it from her gently, watching the red tape closely, as though it would give me a nasty burn if my hand got anywhere near it. I felt the metal, warm and smooth in my fingers. Somewhere, someone behind me shouted 'Go!' and Honey leapt into a canter.

I watched the egg jiggle with every one of Honey's strides. Stay put! I ordered it. Just stay put!

I could make out Carly on my right, setting up Destiny for the first pole. It looked as though she was a nose in front. But only a nose.

I tightened my grip on the reins and held the spoon a little further away, shifting my weight in the saddle and leaning slightly to the right. I neck-reined, pressing the reins against the left side of Honey's neck and, responding to my commands, Honey bent right around the first pole. We cantered on to the second pole. I used the same commands on the opposite side and she bent left. That was the easy part. The third pole, the one we had to twist all the way around, was coming up.

We cantered towards the pole. I could see Destiny ahead of us, see her shoes flashing silver in the sunlight. There was no chance of us winning now, not with Carly so far ahead. I heard the voices of the Shady Creek riders shouting and screaming, all mixed up like waves crashing. The egg jiggled and jiggled, teasing me.

I held tight to the reins. I'd never neck-reined such a tight turn before. Then it all made sense. Everything I'd learned at the Grove, everything about dressage and communicating with my horse, all those leg aids, didn't just apply in the dressage arena. Alex, my dressage coach, had been right. The skills Honey and I had learned could help us ride better in any type of competition.

I sat as deep as I could, holding on tight to the spoon, and applied pressure with my right leg just behind Honey's girth. With the pressure of my left leg on the girth, the reins against the right side of her neck and my weight, Honey twisted neatly around the pole.

We bent through the poles again and cantered towards the finish line. Destiny made it back first, half a length in front. Carly yowled with delight and turned immediately in the saddle to gauge my reaction. I was stoked, grinning at my team-mates as though we'd just won the gold medal in the three-day event.

'What are you so happy about?' Becky asked, slapping Charlie's neck. 'We lost.'

I watched the Creeps celebrate their victory, high-fiving each other and sending unsavoury gestures in our direction. Normally it would have eaten me up. Normally I'd be reaching for something to eat! But this time was different.

'Yeah, we lost,' I said, tossing our team's egg and spoon in Gary's fruit box. 'But we won, too.'

Julie wrinkled her nose. 'That's so weird.'

Jodie nodded, leaning forward to scratch Buttons's ears. 'Totally.'

'We're a team,' I said, the joy of it all bursting

inside me. 'It's the four of us together from now on. Isn't that what we've always wanted?'

'Well, yeah,' Becky said.

'So let's get out there,' I said as Gary placed the first plastic bottle down on an upturned garbage bin, 'and kick some serious rump.'

'One for all,' Julie said, offering her hand.

'And all for one.' Jodie slapped her hand down on top of her sister's.

Becky raised an eyebrow and added her hand to the pile, a smile playing at the corners of her mouth.

I laughed aloud and leaned forward, gathering them all up in a horseback-hug. Honey snorted and stamped. 'Okay, okay, one for you, too!'

I collapsed over her neck and wrapped my arms tightly around her. Win or lose, it didn't get much better than this.

Three

Horseshoe Shuffle

'How d'you reckon she'll take to her new pair of dancing shoes, Ash?' Kevin O'Connor, Shady Creek's number one farrier, winked up at me. It was a cool morning but what seemed like rivers of sweat rolled down his round red face and dripped onto the dust. It was probably warm under the huge leather apron he was wearing. And I suppose holding up a whole horse by her near foreleg was enough to make anyone a little hot under the headcollar.

'Am I doing a good job?' I asked, eyeing up Kevin's toolbox. It was almost as big as me and bursting with shoeing hammers, pincers (which look like a huge pair of tweezers) and pritchels (hot horseshoe hole-makers) — all essential horse pedicure equipment.

'You're the best horse-holder I've come across in a long while.'

It was up to me to hold Honey as still as possible whenever the farrier paid her a visit. Holding my Honey horse is always unreal, but what I really wanted to do was get my hands on Kevin's rasp (a cross between a chisel and a horsy nail file) and give her a makeover myself. I wondered for a moment how she'd look with brightly painted feet — maybe red or gold, or blue for Shady Creek Riding Club. No more of that black hoof oil — boring!

'Can I help?'

Kevin clipped the clenches (the nail ends) on Honey's old shoe with his buffer then wiggled the shoe loose with a pair of pincers starting from her heel. He moved along the branches (the sides) of her shoe then pulled it off backwards. Her foot looked odd, much smaller, now that it was shoeless. 'You are helping.'

'Maybe when you're finished with Honey I could come with you? Hold the other horses or something? My fees are really competitive.'

'Competitive?' Kevin laughed aloud as he trimmed Honey's hoof. Chunks of her foot fell to the ground like clipped toenails. 'Is that so?'

'I don't want to brag but I know a lot about money.' I held fast to Honey's halter while Kevin tidied up her newly trimmed foot with the rasp I'd had my eye on.

'You do, eh?' Kevin tried a fullered shoe, a shoe with a groove that would help with grip, on Honey's foot. The shoe was too big. Kevin chose a smaller size — it was almost perfect, so he lowered Honey's foot gently to the ground and beat it for a minute or two against his anvil. One more try and it was just right.

'As a matter of fact, I do, and if you ever need any odd jobs done I'm the kid to call.'

'I'll keep it in mind.' Kevin wiped his brow on his shirtsleeve and rummaged in his toolbox.

'She's like Cinderella with her brand-new shoes, eh, Kevin?' I said. 'Except she'd have to haul her own carriage to the ball.'

Kevin laughed, then stuffed a handful of nails into his mouth and hammered them into Honey's foot one by one. He twisted off and bent down the ends to make clenches, which would hold the shoe on tight.

'All done,' Kevin said, placing Honey's newly shod hoof on the ground. He stood up, stretching his back.

I patted Honey's neck again and again, praising her for being such a good girl. She nuzzled my hand, searching for a treat.

'You know me too well,' I murmured, pulling a carrot out of the back pocket of my jeans. Honey crunched it up in two bites. I led her to the paddock, where a pair of magpies were arguing in a bottlebrush tree, and she wandered off to test out her new silver shoes.

While Kevin packed his gear into the back of his dusty ute, I ran to the house and upstairs to the 'bank'. I'm proud to say that I take care of Honey myself. I buy her feed, pay her vet and farrier bills and even spoil her with the occasional treat, like tail bandages or a bag of horse licorice. Every cent of the prize money from the Waratah Grove Junior Cross-Country Riding Championships and whatever I earn from doing odd jobs and selling ribbon browbands (I make my own called 'Bandies') I spend on Honey and that suits me just fine.

'You'd better not be wearing those riding boots of yours in your room again, Ashleigh Louise!' Dad's voice boomed up the stairs after me. He'd been sitting at the kitchen table madly scribbling something on a piece of paper when I'd burst in. It was one of his rare days off from Shady Creek and Districts Hospital where he works as the Nurse Unit Manager. It's pretty cool having a nurse dad. Unless of course you're sick — then it's no use at all. Nurse dads have seen really sick people and usually aren't as sympathetic to their own kids.

'No, Dad,' I yelled back, opening up my Horse Cents jar and frantically trying to think up an excuse for lying. I counted out enough notes to pay Kevin and ran downstairs again before Dad could figure out that not only had I been wearing those riding boots of mine in my room again, I'd sat on my bed in my grubbiest jeans and stolen the last carrot from the veggie crisper in the fridge.

Kevin and I made a date for six weeks' time before he heaved himself into his ute, rattled down the driveway and drove off in the direction of his next job. Just as I had settled myself under my favourite tree to watch Honey and think about how gorgeous she is I heard a whistle. The noise was so loud and so shrill, at first I thought there was a fire. I leapt to my feet, my heart pounding.

'Ash, Ash!'

I spun around. Was the house on fire? Would I have to rescue Dad and my collection of horse books, photos of Honey and horsy memorabilia? And what about my trophies? And my headless horse clock? There was no doubt in my mind. No matter what his condition, Dad would just have to help me carry all that stuff out.

Dad was hanging out of the back door, our kitchen door, waving at me with both arms. He blew his whistle again, louder. I had the sudden urge to wrench it from his mouth and make a few Ashleigh-style modifications to it with Kevin's shoeing hammer.

'Baby drill!' Dad hollered, his whistle still wedged in his mouth. 'All hands on deck.'

I groaned and slapped my hands to my forehead. This couldn't be happening. Again! I peeked through my fingers at the back door. Yep. He was really there, and blowing that whistle louder than ever. I summoned all my courage and peeked again, into Flea's place this time. All I needed was for him to re-enact Dad's baby drill for every member of Shady Creek Primary School on Monday. Phew. He was nowhere to be seen.

'Ash, now!' Dad was hopping from foot to foot, tapping his watch. 'The clock is ticking, kiddo!'

I sighed and dragged myself to the door wondering what I had ever done to deserve the baby drill.

Dad pressed a button on his watch. 'One minute and thirty-eight seconds, Ash. That's nowhere near your best time,' he said, frowning and scratching at his beard.

I stared up at him. He looked like the Dad I used to know. The red hair, freckles and blue eyes were still there. But that was about it. Just the outer shell. On the inside he was a ticking baby bomb.

'Stand up straight!' Dad barked. 'Eyes front, hands by your sides. Good! What is your mission?'

I rolled my eyes. 'Dad, it's only a baby.'

'What is your mission?' Dad folded his arms across his chest and raised one ginger-coloured eyebrow.

'It's not even born yet.'

Dad scowled. 'Your mission!'

'Dad, yes, Dad!' I sighed, saluting him. 'To locate the packed bags and the camera and load them into the car.'

Dad smiled. 'Excellent! Now check your position.'

I groaned. 'I know where I'm standing.'

'Your position!' Dad pointed at the back of the kitchen door.

'This is so weird.' I tapped the floor plan of the house, which Dad had pinned to the door. He'd spent hours drawing it up on the computer and had laminated it at work. Every room, every nook and every cranny of the house, both upstairs and downstairs, was carefully labelled. He'd even stuck a photo of my face where the hospital bags were kept, just in case I forgot my mission in all the excitement. 'I hope my sister is worth it.'

'On your marks!' Dad reset his stopwatch. 'Get set!' His finger was poised over the button. 'Go!'

I realised then I had a choice. I could hit Dad with my world-famous telepathic powers and he'd suddenly order me to saddle up Honey and go for a hack. Or I could make a mad dash for the cupboard under the stairs, grab the hospital bag and gallop to the car like I was being chased by a herd of stampeding zebras.

Forty-three seconds later I was slumped over the bonnet of the car gulping sweet air into my lungs.

Dad examined his stopwatch and beamed. 'That was a top run, Ash. You shaved point two of a second off your last time.'

'Tell me again why we're doing this?' I asked as we walked back towards the house.

Dad sighed, as though I'd asked the most obvious question in the history of obvious questions. 'We've been through this a million times, Ash.'

I frowned. If there's one thing I can't stand in the whole big wide entire world it's exaggeration. 'It hasn't been a million.'

'Ashleigh, we're having a baby in two weeks. Mum and I need you to help out as much as you can.'

'I do so help out. I groom Honey. I feed her and take her on hacks. And I pick up her poo, all by myself.'

It was Dad's turn to frown. 'Helping out with Honey is not the kind of help I'm talking about.

Mum'll need you to pitch in around the house when the baby comes. It's all part of being in a family.'

It was then I realised something was missing. 'Where is Mum, by the way?'

Dad hung his whistle on the peg near the door where all the keys are supposed to go. (I say 'supposed' because most mornings Mum is digging behind lounge cushions looking for her keys and Dad is reminding her that if she'd just use the peg she wouldn't lose them in the first place.) 'Work.'

My mouth dropped open. 'In her condition?'

Dad gave me a look. 'There's nothing wrong with being active while you're pregnant, Ashleigh.'

'Active, yes. But installing toilets?'

Dad looked sheepish. 'She likes her job.'

'Mum's carrying pipes around and I have to do the baby drill?'

Dad held out his arms and gave me his number one smile. I let myself be scooped into a cuddle. 'It's all part of being in a family, Ash.'

I snuggled into Dad's chest, so deep and still I could feel his heart beat against my cheek. 'As long as I get my sister.'

'There's a fifty per cent chance.'

'Only fifty?' Fifty wasn't good enough for me. No matter how hard I tried I just couldn't imagine a little boy in my life. No, I was going to have a sister. A sister to laugh with and ride with and go shopping for new joddies with. It was going to be awesome. 'Did I tell you I've got a name picked out?'

Dad held me at arm's length, a smile playing at his lips. 'Oh, have you now?'

'Yep.' I smiled up at him.

'And what, pray tell, do you propose we call our baby?'

'Well, it's going to be a girl and she's going to love horses like me, right?'

'Fifty per cent, Ash.'

'Falabella! Isn't that a great name for a girl?'

Dad shook his head, mystified. 'What on earth is a Falabella?'

I shook my head, disgusted at his complete and total ignorance of one of the most important facts on the planet. 'They're the smallest horses in the world. They average 8.2 hands high. Can you imagine that?'

Dad looked at me like I'd just dropped out of the sky and was speaking gobbledyhoof. 'You are really something.'

'One of a kind,' I said, smiling.

Dad laughed, holding out his arms again. 'Thank goodness!'

I snuggled back into position against his chest.

Four

Baby Love

'Year Six, settle down!'

Our teacher, Mr Morgan, tapped his whiteboard marker on his desk, and sent a stern look at the Creeps' table where Flea was swinging back and forth on his chair balancing a pencil on his top lip. Ryan was hooting with laughter like he'd never seen anything so funny in his life.

'I wish he wouldn't tell us all to settle down,' Becky muttered, scribbling the sums on the board into her Math book. Her long black hair swished on the page. 'It's not as if we're doing anything wrong.'

'Be nice, Rebecca,' I said, ignoring Becky's instant

scowl at the sound of her full name. I ruled a neat red margin down the left side of the page with her ruler. 'You try teaching the Creeps algorithms.'

Becky shrugged. 'I guess.'

'And you should show anyone called "Morgan" the utmost respect.'

Becky put down her pen and raised one eyebrow. 'How come?'

I patted her hand. 'Becky, Becky, Becky.'

'You'd better cut out the Becky, Becky, Becky stuff and just tell me why before I—'

'Mr Morgan … the Morgan horse? Any truly totally horse mad kid worth their molasses would know that there's a chance our teacher could be related to the one and only Thomas Justin Morgan, first owner of Justin Morgan, founder of the American Morgan breed.'

'Is there anything you don't know about horses?' Becky shook her head slowly, wide-eyed.

'Yep.'

'Like what?'

'Like why Destiny doesn't chuck Carly off into the nearest garbage bin and head for the hills.'

Becky giggled. 'This is the hills.'

There was a knock. Twenty-four pairs of eyes flicked to the classroom door. Mrs Jacobs, the school secretary, poked her head inside. She's a whole lot more than a school secretary, though. She answers the phones and types up all the notes that go home from school like regular secretaries. But she's also the best nurse, lost lunchbox finder, money for the phone lender and soggy kindy kid cleaner-upper there is in the universe.

'Can I borrow Ashleigh Miller for a second, please, Mr Morgan?'

Mr Morgan nodded, sighing, then went back to his algorithms.

My stomach tightened. Was I in trouble? I couldn't be. I hadn't done anything even a little bit naughty in ages. Had I forgotten my lunch again? No, we'd already had lunch.

'Chop-chop, Ash!' Mrs Jacobs said, beaming.

I looked to Becky for guidance. She gave me a smile and squeezed my hand. I slipped outside the room and into the corridor, twenty-three pairs of eyes following my every move.

Mrs Jacobs closed the door behind me. 'I have some news.'

44

My heart fluttered. What could it be? Had Honey run away? Had Carly been made the president of the school board? 'What is it? What's wrong?'

'Nothing's wrong. It's great news!' Mrs Jacobs held up a piece of yellow paper. She had a smile on her face so humongous anyone would have thought that the 'International Secretaries Go Home and Don't Come Back to Work for a Week on Full Pay Day' had just been declared. 'Your father just called the office. It seems that you're a big sister!'

'I'm a what?'

'A big sister.' Mrs Jacobs smiled again. 'Isn't that wonderful?'

'Are you sure?'

Mrs Jacobs nodded. 'Positive. I spoke to your dad not ten minutes ago.'

'What is it?'

'It's a baby, dear,' Mrs Jacobs said, patting at her curly brown hair.

'I mean, is it a girl?' I crossed my fingers, toes and legs, just to be sure.

Mrs Jacobs squinted at the piece of yellow paper. 'You know, dear, I was so excited I forgot to ask.' She shrugged and headed off down the corridor. 'Now remember, it's straight to the hospital after school.'

I stood in the corridor alone for a few minutes then opened the classroom door and slipped inside. I slid into my chair and sat there with my mouth hanging open and my eyes popping out.

Becky looked me over for a second. 'What's with you?'

'I . . . I . . .'

Becky frowned. 'Are you okay? You're acting a bit weird.'

'It's . . . I . . . sis—'

Becky raised that eyebrow again. 'Are you trying to tell me something? English would help.'

I swallowed, hard. 'B–baby. Born to-today.'

'WOW!' Becky jumped out of her seat. 'Congratulations, Ash.'

'Is there something you need to tell us, Ashleigh?' Mr Morgan asked.

I nodded and stood up, clearing my throat. 'I'm a sister!'

'Ash!' Dad pulled me into his arms in the foyer of Shady Creek and Districts Hospital. He squeezed me tight. As much as I love my dad and his cuddles, I could do without the scritchy-scratchy facial hair!

'Icarnbreeve!'

Dad let me go. I gagged, clutching at my throat. 'Thanks for choking me!'

Dad's eyes were damp. 'I'm sorry, I — wow, you're so . . . big!'

He looked at me for a moment. He'd never looked so happy. His face was glowing, like something inside him had been switched on.

'Ash, I just love you, kiddo!'

'I love you, too, Dad.'

Dad grabbed my hand and pulled a white and blue hanky out of the pocket of his jeans, dabbing it against his cheeks. 'Ready to come and meet Baby?'

'Am I ever!' I felt all fizzy. This was the moment I'd longed for, wished for. Being an only child had been great most of the time. I had Mum and Dad all to myself. Nobody fought with me over the remote control (except Dad). I could spend as much time as I wanted in the bath. But something had been missing all these years. My sister!

I followed Dad through a maze of doors, corridors and nurses' stations until we reached the far side of the hospital. It was dim and quiet. Curtains were drawn and people spoke softly. It smelled of washing powder and disinfectant.

Dad stopped outside a door. He turned to me and switched on a huge smile again. 'This is it!'

Dad pushed the door open and stepped aside for me. I took a step in. It was a small room with a bed and a neat chest of drawers. There was a window, but I couldn't see what was outside as the curtains were drawn. There was a sink and another door and a few chairs by the bed. In the corner was a comfy-looking armchair and in the armchair was the most stunning woman I had ever seen gazing at the small bundle in her arms as though it were the most perfect being ever created. I shouldn't be here, I thought. I felt out of place, like an intruder, like an elephant trying to perform *haute école* alongside an Andalusian.

The woman looked up at me with a smile that radiated light.

'Ash,' she said.

I was gobsmacked. When had my mother become this beautiful?

'I'd like to introduce you to your brother.'

Suddenly, with that terrible, that horrible word, the light seemed to fade leaving nothing behind but black despair.

A brother!

I slumped into the nearest chair. I couldn't speak. How could this have happened? How could Mum and Dad do this to me?

A brother!

'Ash, what is it?' Dad laid his hand on my shoulder. I looked up at him.

'It's just ...' I began. How could I say it when they both looked so happy?

I wasn't happy. All I knew about brothers I'd learned from the Terrible Twins, Jenna's brothers. Memories of them swam through my head. Like the time they shoved jelly babies so far up their own noses at my ninth birthday party that Mum had to call an ambulance. Like the time they emptied their ant farm into Jenna's underwear drawer. Like the time they tipped their plates of spaghetti bolognaise into Jenna's school bag when Mrs Dawson was on the phone. And all this was ahead of me!

'Do you want a hold?' Mum said softly.

'I ...'

'Go on, Ash.' Dad scooped the baby out of Mum's arms and placed him gently in mine.

I'd never held a baby before. I didn't know what to do so I sat there all stiff, terrified I might drop him or squeeze too hard. Terrified he'd throw up on my school uniform.

Mum laughed gently. 'Ash, relax. Pretend you're riding.'

I looked down at the bundle in my arms — my brother. He was asleep. His tiny rosebud mouth sucked on his forefinger. His ears were like two delicate pink petals. His eyes were puffy and his hair was sticky and dark. He smelled new. He was warm. Then he yawned and stretched his fingers and I fell in love. All my disappointment washed away. I had a few things to say to him but I was lacking one rather crucial detail.

'What's his name?'

Mum and Dad clasped hands for a moment, looking into each other's eyes (okay, so we had a new baby but that's no excuse for romance!).

'Jason,' Mum murmured.

I raised my eyebrows at my parents who were staring at my new brother as though he were a million-dollar yearling. 'Jason? How'd you come up with that?'

'Remember how Honey's old owners called her Argonaut?' Dad said.

'I'm trying to put it behind me, actually.'

'Well that reminded us of Jason and the Argonauts and the name just grew on us.'

'Who and the whats?' Had they developed a new secret language while I was at Waratah Grove? Or did having babies do this to everyone?

Mum rolled her eyes. 'Jason and the Argonauts. From ancient Greek mythology.'

I stared at her blankly, hoping that whatever was doing this to her would wear off.

'It frightens me what being horse mad has done to your education, Ashleigh Louise. As of today you read nothing but Homer.'

'Homer?'

Mum dropped her face into her hands. 'Grant, what have we created?'

Dad tugged at my ponytail. 'Homer. As in Trojan Horse.'

'Horses,' I said, grinning. Finally they were speaking a language I understood. 'Cool!'

Soon it was time for Dad and me to go, but I'd managed to explain to Jason the origins of the modern horse, from eohippus to equus, before he decided that learning about the horse's transition from toes to hooves was much less interesting than screaming his head off.

We arrived home in time to find Becky, a huge bunch of flowers, a small red envelope and an invitation to dinner at Rebecca's Garden on our doorstep.

'It's a boy?' Becky said, wrapping her arms around my neck. 'That's too bad, Ash.'

I thought about Jason, his face, his tiny wrinkly fingers and mouth that sucked in his sleep.

'He's perfect,' I said. 'He's my brother and he's perfect!'

I gave Becky another quick hug and ran to the paddock to tell Honey my news.

Five

Shady Trails Riding Ranch

Jason had been home for a week when I got the call. It was a little hard to hear what the lady on the other end of the line was saying with all the screaming (from Jason, not the lady). But I was pretty sure I was due to start work at Wavy Tails Hiding Branch this weekend.

The journey home was hard for Honey. She'd come such a long way since I'd found her abandoned, starving and half-dead from the worst case of worms our local vet, Amanda Filano, had ever seen. She'd improved physically. She'd regained condition. She'd become a champion again. But Waratah Grove had taught me that she still bore the scars, physical and mental, of her treatment before Becky and I had stumbled across her on that afternoon hack so long ago.

It had been many months since I'd last ridden down that dirt road. I had never wanted to see it again and I knew from her reaction that Honey felt the same. The closer we came to her old home the more frightened Honey grew. She snorted, tossed her head and finally stopped dead, refusing to go any further. She didn't understand that horrors no longer awaited her. I pushed her forward. She took a step, then another, then went into reverse, just as she had done in the dressage arena at Waratah Grove.

I knew what was wrong with her. She was afraid. Honey's nature, like any horse, was telling her to run from danger as fast as she could. Her rider was forcing her towards it and she was torn. Her back arched. I could feel her curling up, ready to lash out with her legs.

I scrambled out of the saddle and held her head, stroking her nose. Her eyes rolled and she leapt back again. I held her tighter.

'It's all right, girl,' I murmured. 'Everything's gonna be all right.'

I knew what I had to do. A smile played at my lips thinking of Lena, the smallest member of my cabin at the Grove, who'd taught me so much about horses. I prepared Honey to 'park'.

The idea was to remind her to trust me, to remind her that she moved on my command, not because she was afraid.

I held tight to Honey's reins. She pulled back. I brought her forward. She lurched sideways and I brought her back. She took a step forward. Then another. I pushed her back again. Then, instantly, she settled. It was like someone had flicked a switch in her brain and she'd remembered that I'd never hurt her. She remembered to believe in me and that I'd never let her down.

I stroked her neck again and again until I was sure. Then I mounted gently, settling into the saddle as steadily as I had lowered Jason into his crib the night before.

Honey was calmer. I just had to get her to Wavy Tails and I was sure she'd be fine. I rode her quietly, focussing on her, reading her. I knew it was ahead, but I didn't know what to expect. What did the place look like now? Who had I spoken to? What kind of name for a riding school was Wavy Tails, anyway?

We rode to the top of a small hill then paused. Looking down, what looked to me to be the horsy equivalent of Disneyland had landed where there had once stood a dusty paddock, an abandoned shack and an empty water tank.

I gasped. It was totally unbelievable. There were round yards, green green paddocks, a holding yard and an arena — and that was just for starters! There was also a large horseshoe-shaped building, which wrapped around a holding yard where I could just make out about five horses saddled, ready and waiting for their riders to arrive.

We rode down the hill and stood at the entrance to the property. In place of the rusty old gate and padlock there stood a tall, proud red-brick archway, with Shady Trails Riding Ranch (definitely a better name than Wavy Tails Hiding Branch) in huge gold letters across the top. Honey didn't hesitate. It was like she knew this place was built for horses and she was going to be safe.

We took our first steps onto Shady Trails territory. There was a real road stretching out ahead of us from the gate a few hundred metres to the riding school itself. On my right was a newly fenced paddock. Half a dozen horses grazed peacefully, in such stark contrast to Honey's experiences here that I shivered. On my left there was a car park, and a sign that read *Horses Only Past This Point*.

'Wow,' I said. 'Double and triple and quadruple wow!'

Honey and I followed the road to a brand-new brick building. It was the main complex. There were signs pointing to reception, a café, washrooms, a gear and souvenir shop, and a party room. My mouth fell open. I'd never seen anything like it — not in the city, not even at Waratah Grove.

I pulled Honey up outside reception and dismounted, my bottom lip still hitting the floor. I didn't know what to do or where to go. I didn't even know who I'd spoken to (thanks, Jason!). I was spinning in a slow, stunned circle, clinging to Honey's reins when the reception door opened.

'Good morning.'

I stopped spinning. 'I'm Ashleigh. Ashleigh Miller.'

A very elegant lady with silver hair cropped to her chin and neat, expensive-looking riding clothes stood in the doorway. 'It's great to meet you in person, Ashleigh. We spoke on the phone. My name is Mrs McMurray.'

Mrs McMurray held out her hand and I shook it. 'This is Honey,' I said. 'She used to—'

Mrs McMurray nodded. 'I know. I've heard all about what happened here.' She smiled and reached out to Honey, gently stroking the tip of her nose. 'I hope Shady Trails makes it up to her.'

'It's awesome!' I said. I felt like I would burst. 'It's totally awesome.'

Mrs McMurray laughed. 'It's not too bad. Come and I'll show you round. But first we'll find a spot to rest and water your Honey.'

I followed Mrs McMurray to a road-width gap in the horseshoe building. It was a tunnel leading through to the holding yard. The walls were glass. I could see straight into the café on one side and the party room on the other. It was perfect for horse mad kids. I could have cried. Why wasn't there anything like this for me when I was a kid? I mean, I was going to be twelve in a few months. What if I was too old for this stuff now? Hang on a minute, I thought. I was determined — I would NEVER be too old for horses. Horses are my life — always have been, always will be. I paused for a moment, gazing through the glass walls into the party room. I could see it now — my party, my birthday, with all my very best friends and most of all, with my Honey horse.

It was all amazing. There were tables in the shape of horseshoes, yes, horseshoes! The walls were painted with huge bright murals, all with horses — brumbies galloping through glittering snow; delicate Arabs dressed in traditional attire; horses of fantasy, myth and legend. Silver unicorns hung from the ceiling. Horsy party hats were set up on the tables. There was a throne for the birthday girl or boy, the back of which was in the shape of Pegasus with wings outstretched, ready to fly.

'Wow,' I said. It was all I could say.

'Like it?' Mrs McMurray said. She sounded hopeful.

I nodded. 'Who wouldn't?'

'We thought the kids in the party room would like to watch the comings and goings of the horses. Then we thought that the parents in the café might like to watch their kids.'

'Wow,' I said again.

'I think she'll be comfy over here, lovey.'

I led Honey, following Mrs McMurray across the holding yard into a bright clean stable.

'We can house twenty horses in here at any one time,' Mrs McMurray said.

'Wow.' I thought I'd have to pinch myself. I mean, we were in Shady Creek where Gary's home-made cross-country course, which he'd knocked together with used tyres and old doors painted to look like brick walls, was the most sophisticated thing I'd ever experienced at Riding Club.

'She's cooled out after our walk, so why don't you untack her, give her a quick rub down and give her a feed and a roll?' Mrs McMurray opened a stall door for Honey and before I led her inside, I noticed the name above the stall: *Honey*.

'Wow!'

Mrs McMurray laughed again. 'I'm guessing you approve.'

'This place is so cool. Everyone is gonna love it here!'

Mrs McMurray smiled. She leaned on the stall door and looked around her. 'It has turned out well, hasn't it?'

I nodded, unbuckling Honey's girth.

'I always wanted to open a riding school of my own. Always. And this is just the way I hoped it would be.' Mrs McMurray stroked Honey's nose again. I hoisted her saddle from her back and flicked her saddle blanket onto the wall of the stall. Her coat was wet and sticky although the weather was cool. She had been carrying an eleven-going-on-twelve-year-old, though.

'Is this the first riding school you've had?' I asked. I unbuckled Honey's bridle and slipped it up over her ears and down her nose. The bit jingled as she let it fall from her mouth.

Mrs McMurray nodded. 'Sure is.'

'Well, for a beginner you're doing really well,' I said, rubbing Honey's back and sides with a clean, dry cloth.

Mrs McMurray laughed aloud. 'Thanks, love.'

I was curious. 'What did you do before? You know, before Shady Trails?'

'I was a teacher,' she said. 'History. Big kids.'

'History.' I pulled a face. 'Ugh.'

'What do you mean "ugh"? If it wasn't for History we'd know nothing about the works of Xenophon.'

I hung up my cloth and patted Honey before sliding open the stall door bolt. 'Xylophone?'

'Xenophon! He wrote one of the first known books on horses nearly 2,500 years ago in Greece.' Mrs McMurray looked like she couldn't decide between being shocked at my ignorance or wildly enthusiastic about Mr Xenophon.

'Why don't you teach at the big school in town?' I watched as Honey dipped her head into her drinking trough and took a long cool sip of water.

Mrs McMurray frowned. Her face darkened for a split second and just for that moment I was afraid I'd said something really awful.

'No, I—' she began. 'My life is here now. Teaching is in the past.'

I felt horrible. Something wriggled in my stomach and my face and ears grew hot.

'Come and meet the horses,' Mrs McMurray said. I was relieved to change the subject. 'I'm so happy you were able to start today and get to know the place, love. Our very first customers are coming in for a pony lead tomorrow and you look perfect for the job.'

'Everything looks great!' I said. 'It sounds great!'

'Hey, Mrs Mac.'

I twisted around. Standing behind me in a red Shady Trails Riding Ranch polo shirt, black joddies and black boots was a young woman, who looked about twenty, with long curly blonde hair tied in a messy ponytail and a smile as bright as those in a toothpaste commercial. I liked her at once.

'Ashleigh, this is Samantha, one of our stablehands,' Mrs McMurray said.

Samantha stuck out her hand. I took it and we shook.

'It's Sam, actually. No one but my gran calls me Samantha. Oh, and my old school principal.' Sam gave me a wink.

'Well, I'm Ash, actually,' I said.

'And I'm Aaron.'

A young man, about the same age as Sam, with carrot-coloured hair and very blue eyes set down the wheelbarrow full of horse manure he was pushing and wiped his sweaty forehead on his sleeve. His shirt was identical to Sam's. He cast Sam a sideways glance, which she didn't seem to notice, and set off through the stables to the holding yard.

'Samantha, sorry, Sam, love, would you show Ash around?' Mrs McMurray said, looking at her watch. 'I have an appointment with a graphic artist who's going to be designing our brochure.'

Sam grinned and slapped Mrs McMurray's arm. 'No probs, Mrs Mac.'

Mrs McMurray smiled at me and rubbed her arm. 'Enjoy the rest of your first day, Ash. Sam, organise a uniform for Ash, will you, love? I have to get back to the office.' With that Mrs McMurray walked away.

A uniform of my own? How cool! Shady Trails was my first real job and I couldn't wait to get started.

'Have you met the horses?' Sam said, leaning over the stall door to rub Honey's mane.

'Not yet,' I said. 'But I'm totally dying to.'

'C'mon,' Sam said, indicating the holding yard with her hand. I followed her to the stable doors. 'Shady Trails has some of the best school horses I've seen and I've worked in heaps of places. Mrs McMurray really knows what she's doing when it comes to buying horses.'

We stepped out into the sunlight of the holding yard. There were five horses, saddled and waiting, their reins secured to the fence with pieces of twine.

There was a gorgeous, sweet-faced bay mare with huge, gentle dark brown eyes who looked to be about 13 hands high.

Sam unlooped the twine attached to her reins and patted her neck. 'This is Calypso. Want to ride her?'

'Do I?' I gasped. 'Of course!'

'She's yours for the day. Hop on board and we'll take you on a tour of Shady Trails.'

I slid my helmet back over my head and buckled it then gathered the reins at Calypso's shoulder, put my left foot in the stirrup and bounced into the saddle.

'How does it feel?' Sam said, smiling.

I grinned. 'Great. Unreal. Bit weird, though. I haven't ridden any other horse but Honey since I got her.'

'Honey won't mind. And you need to test yourself on other horses — keep your skills up.' Sam untied the loops of twine around the reins of a taller chestnut mare and mounted, looking as comfortable in the saddle as she would in a banana lounge. 'This is Penny, well, Penelope really. She's my favourite.'

I leaned over and rubbed the mare's forelock. She closed her eyes and drooped her head with pleasure. She was very like Honey in the looks department with white socks, a honey-coloured coat and a white blaze, but she had the thickest mane I'd ever seen on a horse her size. It looked like a shaggy pony had dropped his mane and she'd decided it looked good on her.

'We're just waiting on—' Sam began.

Aaron burst into the holding yard buckling up his helmet and frantically untied the twine on another horse's reins.

'You're late.' Sam frowned. 'Ash and I are busy women.'

Aaron's face flushed a colour similar to his hair. 'I'll just get Hector organised.'

'Hector?' I wondered aloud.

'Mrs McMurray named him. She names all the horses,' Sam said. 'You ready, Azz?'

Aaron nodded, adjusting his girth strap with the speed of someone who'd clearly done it all his life.

'Let's rock 'n' roll!' Sam led the way through a gate on the far side of the holding yard. The stables were on our left, the rest of the horseshoe-shaped building on our right. Behind us was a path with a sign, like a street sign. Right pointed to the arena and round yards and left pointed to the trails.

'Take your pick, Ash,' Sam said.

'I'll take it all, thanks.' How could I choose? I wanted to see everything.

'Why don't we take Ash past the arena then down to the trails from there?' Aaron said from behind me.

'A brilliant suggestion, as usual, Azz.' Sam grinned mischievously.

Aaron's face burned again.

I followed Sam right, in the direction of the arena. Calypso was a smooth, easy ride. I held my reins in one hand and scratched her mane with the other. I looked around. There were more paddocks and horses grazing. Sam pointed out Clarence, Mrs McMurray's great bay gelding.

After the tour was over, I collected Honey and my brand-new Shady Trails uniform. My first day at Shady Trails had been unbelievable. I couldn't wait to come back tomorrow.

Six

Saddle Sores

'It's unimaginable, unbelievable, inconceivable!' I told Becky at school on Monday.

'That good, huh?' Becky shoved a low-lying branch out of the way as we ducked under our tree. It was lunchtime and the playground was a mad rush of soccer balls, skipping ropes, elastics and crying kindergarteners.

'Better than good,' I chattered. 'Better than better than good.'

Becky and I slumped against our tree and ripped the lids off our lunchboxes, automatically eyeing off each other's contents.

'Would it kill them to make me a chicken roll?'

Becky moaned. 'I've never had a single lunch at school that didn't involve chopsticks.'

Becky had been given her usual leftover Chinese feast. My mouth watered just looking at the fried rice and noodles in her lunchbox.

'I'll swap ya?' I offered, holding out my ham and cheese sandwich.

'I'll go you halves,' Becky said.

We shook on it and began munching.

'Did I tell you about my uniform?' I said through a mouthful of sandwich.

'Donchorkivurrmoffull.'

I stared at Becky, my eyebrows raised so high I could feel them hitting my hairline. 'What was that?'

Becky swallowed and took a gulp of orange juice. 'That was, "Don't talk with your mouth full".'

'I'll remember that.' I took another bite of my sandwich and chewed happily. Dad makes the best sandwiches with real butter and cheese and great thick slices of ham. I swallowed it down. 'I did my first pony leads yesterday. You know, at Shady Trails. It was so cool.'

'So was Riding Club.' Becky flicked a grain of rice from her maroon Shady Creek Primary School shorts. 'Especially the part when the Creeps won the potato race.'

'I had this kid and she was so sweet — it was her first ride, you know?'

'But I really loved it when they won the sack race.'

'And then, I got to groom these two ponies called Brandy and Bartok — they are so cute!'

'Me and the twins cheered our heads off when the Creeps kicked our butts in the bottle race.' -

'And then I had to muck out, which was pretty disgusting but you know better than anyone that I love horses enough to love scooping up their poo.'

'But the icing on the cake was when they whipped us in the egg and spoon race.'

'And the stablehands, Azz and Sam are so — the Creeps WHAT?' For the first time since we opened our lunchboxes, I really looked at Becky's face. Her lips were thin and her cheeks were pale. It didn't take a genius to work out how ropable she was.

'Yes, Ash, they creamed us. They smashed us. They totally, utterly bombed us!'

'But why?' I was confused. We'd lost to them once or twice in the past. But not like this.

'Why do you think, Ash?' Becky looked into my eyes, hard.

I shrugged. 'I don't know. I've got no idea.'

'Think about it, Ash. There were four of them and three of us. We have a four-rider team, but one of our riders was missing in action and the stand in from the Under 10s was scared of a pony's shadow.' Becky's face was flushed and her eyes were wide. I'd had no idea she was upset with me.

'I-I'm sorry, Beck. I didn't know. I didn't think.'

'You can say that again.' Becky snapped the lid back onto her lunchbox, her noodles untouched.

I wasn't hungry any more either. I folded up the rest of my sandwich and swished it back into my lunchbox. I felt sick. My tummy squeezed and squeezed. I hate arguments.

'I won't work on Riding Club days, okay?'

Becky snorted. 'That's big of you.'

'I said I'm sorry. I said I won't work on Riding Club days. What more do you want from me?' I was hurt, and starting to get angry. Becky had done all kinds of stuff before, like all those dressage competitions, and I hadn't complained once.

'Can't you see?' Becky said, ducking low to avoid a soccer ball.

I frowned. 'See what?'

Becky rolled her eyes and sighed. 'I don't want Shady Trails here. I've never wanted it. Dad doesn't want it either.'

I was shocked. My jaw dropped faster than a sweaty pony in a patch of made-for-rolling-in grass. 'What are you talking about?'

Becky's face changed. She went from mad as a cut stallion to frightened in under a second. 'Dad and I have talked about it. There's no room in Shady Creek for them and us — for Shady Trails and Riding Club. We'll lose riders and once that happens we'll have to pull the pin.'

I rubbed my forehead with my hands, trying to make sense of what Becky was saying.

'We'll have to close. We need membership fees to stay alive. Shady Creek Riding Club will be history and it'll be all thanks to Shady Trails.' Becky spat out the last two words as if they were venom.

I shook my head, the full meaning of what Becky had just said running through my veins like cold wet concrete. 'What can I do?'

Becky sat up straight. 'Quit. Leave straight away. Help me get people to stay away from Shady Trails.'

I scrunched up my face like a chimpanzee. I thought about Sam and Azz and Mrs McMurray and how much I liked them already. I thought about the little girl on the pony lead and how she'd laughed the whole time and begged her mum to bring her back. Then I thought about the money and everything Honey needed, about Mum who wasn't working now and how much stuff my parents needed to buy for Jason. 'I can't.'

Becky grabbed my hand. 'For me. For us. For Riding Club and Dad and the twins. And how awful would it be to have to join Pinebark Ridge?'

Pinebark Ridge. Our mortal Riding Club enemy.

'I dunno, Beck.'

My best friend squeezed my hand and looked into my eyes. 'Just for me then.'

She was asking a lot of me, maybe too much this time. As we made our way back to class and pulled out our reading books I asked myself over and over again: what would Becky do if she were me?

★ ★ ★

I was starving. It'd been nearly three hours since lunch and I couldn't wait to see what Mum was cooking for dinner. There was nothing better than opening the back door after a long day at school and eating up the smells of a scrummy dinner.

I let myself in the back door. The kitchen was quiet. The oven was off, the stove was off. The microwave was silent and dark, like a lonely cave.

'Mum?' I called. 'Mum?'

I could hear muffled voices and followed them to the lounge room. Mum was on the lounge in her dressing gown and slippers feeding Jason and surrounded by pillows, tissues, cloth nappies and coffee cups. The telly was on and Mum was staring at an American woman who was exploring her feelings in front of a live studio audience.

'What're you doing?'

Mum looked up. She looked like someone who hadn't slept in a very long time. Her eyes were red and there were dark circles under them. She looked at me for a moment then focussed on the TV again.

'Mum?' I said again. 'What's for dinner?'

'Can't you see I'm busy?' she snapped.

I was stung. After my horrible lunch with Becky this was the last thing I needed.

'I'm–I'm just hungry. I've had a bad day.' I wanted to cry. I wanted to curl up beside her on the lounge and rest my head in her lap like I used to. But Jason was there now and there was no room for me.

'I've had a bad day too,' Mum said. 'He doesn't stop crying unless I feed him.'

Mum took a deep breath in and it rattled out of her again. 'I don't know if you've noticed, Ashleigh, but I'm tired. So if you're hungry there's a fridge in the kitchen.'

'When's Dad coming home?' I asked.

Mum closed her eyes and leaned her head back into the lounge. 'Who knows?'

She coughed then sniffed and I realised she was crying. Tears spilled down her pale face and trickled under her chin and down her neck. I had never seen my mother cry. It was awful, the most awful thing ever.

I took a tentative step towards her. 'Mum?' I whispered, scared.

'I'm just so tired.' Mum opened her eyes just a crack and peered down at Jason. He was sleeping at last. I reached out my hands and scooped him up into my arms then placed him gently into the bassinette in the corner. By the time I turned around Mum was asleep as well. I pulled her robe tight around her, took the phone off the hook, switched off the TV and tiptoed out of the room. There was work to be done.

Seven

A Tangled Web

'So what'd you do yesterday?'

I shrugged, not knowing what to say. I wanted to tell Becky all about the grand opening of Shady Trails Riding Ranch, but I just couldn't. I fidgeted with my reins, buckling and unbuckling them. 'Nothing much. Just stayed at home with Mum and Jason.'

I hated lying to her, but I knew how she felt about Shady Trails. I also knew that I didn't want to quit.

'It's just so good you made it today.' Becky glanced over her shoulder at the Creeps, whose ears were practically throbbing, and leaned closer to me. 'We need all the practice we can get before the gymkhana.

I don't want a repeat performance of last meeting. They were unbearable for a week after that.'

It was our last Riding Club meeting before the gymkhana and we had a lot of work to do. For Becky, the twins and me it wasn't about beating Pinebark Ridge (like it usually is!) or any other club. It was all about beating the Creeps, and beating them so hard they crawled back to the rocks they'd been living under.

Becky shifted in her saddle, patting Charlie's neck absentmindedly. The gorgeous bay gelding stood up straight, calm and ready for action. 'Is it just me or are we missing a few people?'

I had a quick look down the line of riders, waiting for their gear and tack to be cleared by Gary. There was no point in denying it. Numbers were down.

'Maybe there's a bug going round,' I said. 'Who knows? Maybe if we're really lucky the bug'll come and bite the Creeps on their butts.'

I had a feeling that our missing riders were trying Shady Trails on for size. I hadn't counted on it, but at least half the members of Riding Club had come to the grand opening. It had been such an incredible day with prizes, a raffle, a colouring-in competition (which I would have loved to have won myself — who wouldn't want an entire day at Shady Trails for free?), music and face painting. I was torn between being stoked for Mrs McMurray that her new riding school was off to such a great start, feeling horrible about helping to sink Gary's Riding Club and being terrified Becky would find out that I'd lied to her. I'd spent most of the night wishing upon every star in the sky that nobody had recognised me in my Shady Trails shirt and if they had, that they were struck down with acute and irreversible memory loss.

Becky glowered at the line.

'Traitors,' she spat. 'None of 'em better even dare show their faces around here again.'

'Ready?' Gary called.

'Yes!' the Shady Creek riders sang in unison.

Gary pushed his scrappy old blue Riding Club cap up on his head and frowned. 'Where is everybody?' It was hard to believe he'd only just noticed. The hole in the line of riders was as obvious as tomato sauce on a wedding dress.

I sank in my saddle, making a point of staring at my pommel.

'Why don't you ask Ashleigh?' piped up a horribly familiar voice.

My tummy flip-flopped. Trust Carly.

Gary looked at me with his eyebrows raised. I swallowed and scratched under my helmet wishing I had a carrot or some crackers or something else particularly crunchy in my hands — I always eat when I'm nervous.

'D-dunno,' I stammered, sending Carly a look that I hoped was at the very least poisonous and at best fatal. 'I hear there's some kind of bug going around.'

'There is,' Carly said. 'It's called Trails fever.'

I prayed, right then and there, for laser beam eyes.

Gary frowned deeper. I could tell he wasn't buying it for a second. 'Must be a new one. One of those super bugs maybe.'

'It's really super,' Flea said, a smirk twisting the corners of his nasty mouth. Scud shook his head. His bit jingled and he snorted with satisfaction. 'Super dooper.'

Ryan whooped like a winded gorilla.

I was bristling, but knowing how much they wanted me to take the bait I clamped my jaw shut. I was sure I hadn't seen them at the opening. But it had been so busy. There had been people and horses everywhere. I'd been on free pony ride duty for the whole day, leading Bartok, Brandy and Paris in a large circle in the top paddock. They'd all worn glittering saddlecloths and looked like equine disco balls. It had been such fun, but I hadn't seen even half the people who'd attended.

'We'll just have to start without them,' Gary said. He looked at his watch then over his shoulder at the gates. 'But I'm sure they'll turn up.'

I stared at my hands, desperate to avoid Becky's eyes. I'd never felt like this before. Sure, I'd felt bad when I'd tried to sell off my mother's wedding dress to raise money to buy a horse. And I'd felt terrible when I'd bought a horse on the Internet and Mum and Dad had had to reimburse the owner's petrol money. But this? It was like there was a big ugly fairy on my shoulder telling me how disappointed she was in me, how much I'd let my best friend down and how ashamed I should be of myself. I realised then what the yucky gnawing feeling was — guilt. Guilt with a capital G.

Gary sent us into the warm-up ring for ten minutes then called us back and ushered us into our teams. The Under 12s were all present and accounted for, as were the Under 14s. But the Under 16s and Opens were so down on numbers that, for the first time since I'd become a member of Shady Creek Riding Club, they had to join forces just to have enough riders to train.

Gary had the field ready. I recognised straight away that we'd be starting with the potato race. I brightened a little at the thought of cantering Honey madly down the course.

Gary had placed a bucket on each team's centre line. At the end of the course was a hula hoop on the grass with five potatoes inside it. One potato sat all by itself at the starting line.

'Does everyone remember the rules?' Gary asked, standing on his beloved plastic milk crate.

There were some 'yeses' and a lot of unintelligible rumblings from the Shady Creek riders.

'Rider One — you will take the lone potato, drop it into the bucket on the centre line and continue down to the Hula hoop.' Gary paused for effect. 'You'll dismount, pick up a potato, mount and gallop back to the starting line where you'll give the potato to the next rider. Got that?'

'Yes!' I called. Flea snored and Carly yawned so wide I could see her tonsils.

'Good,' Gary said. 'Rider One will go out twice by which time all six potatoes should be in the bucket. First team home with all potatoes in their bucket is the winner.'

Julie waved her hand in the air.

'We're not at school, Jodie,' Carly said. 'You look like an idiot putting your hand up like that.'

Julie seethed. As much as she loves her twin she hates being called Jodie, especially when it's done on purpose.

'Yes, Julie,' Gary said. 'And excellent manners, by the way. I hope that some of your fellow riders follow your lead in future.' Gary's eyes fell on Carly, who pretended to be interested in something in Destiny's mane.

'What do we do if we drop the potato?'

'Simple,' Gary said. 'Pick it up and continue the race. The rules clearly state that riders can be mounted or dismounted when picking up dropped potatoes, so do whatever suits you and your horse.'

Becky gave me her most determined face and offered her hand for a high-five. For a moment I forgot all about Shady Trails and lying to Becky and Riding Club numbers being down for the first time ever. I even forgot about the Creeps and how they knew about me and Shady Trails. Until, that is, we were waiting at the starting line, potatoes in hand, and Carly leaned over close enough for only me to hear.

'Win this and I'll talk.'

It was like I'd dived into ice-cold water. My body went numb.

'I don't know what you mean.'

Carly smiled, a mean cruel smile. Her red hair, in its ponytail, snaked down her back. 'I'll spell it out for you then. Throw the race or I'll tell Rebecca's Garden everything about you and Shady Trails and all about your busy day yesterday.'

I gasped. 'How do you know?'

Carly's face twisted into a mask of sheer contempt. 'You're so stupid. Did you really think nobody would ever find out? What planet are you on, Spiller? This is Shady Creek. You're not in the big city any more.'

I looked from Carly's face to my team. Becky punched the air, knock 'em dead-style, and the twins gave me the thumbs up. They were counting on me.

I was Rider One. I was going out twice. I could win it or lose it for them. I thought about Becky and how I was already deceiving her and how much she meant to me. It wasn't worth it.

My eyes met Carly's and I spoke. My voice didn't falter. 'I read you loud and clear.'

Gary rang the bell.

'I can't believe we lost every race,' Becky said at lunchtime. She was shaking her head slowly, mortified. 'This is twice in a row. Twice!'

'Do you get cramps often, Ash?' Julie regarded me with a look I'd never seen before.

I flushed and fidgeted with my cheese and tomato sandwich. 'Um, yeah, quite often. It's the weather, you know?'

'Which leg was it?' Jodie said, squinting at me.

'Right,' I said, rubbing my calf muscle furiously. 'It's really killing me.'

Jodie put down her apple, leaned over and poked at my left leg. 'I was sure you were grabbing your left leg. I remember with—'

'There's always next time. I'm sure it won't happen again.' All I wanted was to drop the subject. I am the world's worst liar. Every time I give it a shot it's like a big neon sign has appeared over my head flashing the words SHE'S LYING in electric purple over and over again. I just can't do it. I don't even want to.

'There won't be a next time,' Becky said, slapping her hands together to shake away some sticky rice.

My tummy dropped into my bottom and I wriggled on the grass. I was caught out! Becky knew I was a rotten faker and she never wanted to talk to me again.

'We only have Riding Club every second Sunday, remember? The gymkhana is on Saturday so there is no next meeting. Next meeting is the gymkhana,' Becky explained.

Phew! I collapsed onto my back sending up thanks to the horse gods and rubbed my eyes, pondering whether all this stress would wind up stunting my growth.

'Can't we get together for some extra training sessions?' Jodie said.

'Twice a week after school should do it,' Becky said. 'But we're all in individual classes as well. Ash, you've signed up for dressage and jumping, haven't you?'

I nodded and rolled onto my tummy. My head was swimming with yucky thoughts that wriggled around like eels snapping at each other. There was no room in there for worrying about training. I heard laughter and looked up. The Creeps were sitting under a tree of their own. Carly was watching me. She waved, a toothy smile plastered from ear to ear, then held up her finger in a 'Number one' gesture. Ryan and Flea did likewise. I made a gesture of my own and buried my head in my arms wishing like nothing else that my life was a DVD and that I could skip over the scenes I didn't like watching.

The rest of the afternoon at Riding Club was a blur. I'd never not loved every second of it. What's not to love — riding my gorgeous Honey horse, spending a whole day in the saddle with Becky by my side, having the most amazing and dedicated instructor I'd ever known? It was all too fantastically amazing to be true. But that day was different. That day everything changed.

Eight

Pree-senting Priyanka

'Can you do me a favour, Ash, lovey?'

I looked up from the pile of poo I was shovelling. Mrs McMurray was leaning on the stall door watching me. She was with a girl about my age whose eyes were so dark they were almost black and whose thick black hair hung down her back in the longest plait I'd ever seen. She smiled and for a second I was so dazzled I didn't notice that she was wearing a red Shady Trails Riding Ranch shirt identical to mine. She had a set of choppers that would make any dentist weep for joy.

'This is Priyanka Prasad.' Mrs McMurray smiled down at her. 'I'd like you to show her the ropes.'

I wiped my hand on my joddies and stretched it out over the stall door. Priyanka grabbed it and we pumped hands. 'No worries, Mrs McMurray.'

Mrs McMurray waved a pile of coloured papers in the air. 'Could you also deliver these for me on your way home, love? Maybe hand them out to your friends at school?'

I squinted at the papers. It looked like the brochures had been printed. In the bottom corner I could just make out a kid in a red shirt. She had two light brown pigtails and a huge grin plastered on her face and looked a terrible lot like me. I was torn between praying Becky would never see a brochure and hoping that the photographer had been kind enough to airbrush out my freckles!

I gulped, then nodded. Maybe I could slip out at night in a black balaclava and poke them into mailboxes, but I could never take them to school.

'Well, Priyanka, I'll leave you in Ash's very capable hands.'

I looked at my hands. They didn't have any capable on them but there sure was a lot of dirt.

'Thanks, Mrs McMurray.' Priyanka flashed one of her smiles. I rubbed at my eyes. Her teeth practically radiated light.

Mrs McMurray left and I leaned on my shovel.

'Reckon you can use a shovel?'

Priyanka raised one eyebrow. 'Reckon I can give it a bash.'

I made a 'welcome in' gesture with my hands and handed Priyanka my shovel. She got stuck into poo detail. I scooped up the dirty straw from the floor with a pitchfork and shook it into the wheelbarrow, replacing it with fresh, clean straw.

'You're good at pooper scooping, Priyanka,' I said, pushing the wheelbarrow to the next stall.

'I should be, I've had enough practice. And it's Pree.'

'Pree?'

'Only my dad calls me Priyanka. He was born in New Zealand. He says "sux" for six and "fet" for fat. He's a doctor. He doesn't believe in shortening names. He reckons if you give a kid a name then you should stick to it. He reckons if you want to call your kid "Bob" do it, but don't call him Robert first.' Pree took a breath.

'Well, that's—' I began.

'Mum calls me Pree, but. And Gran calls me Pree. My friends call me Pree. You know, when I think about it, everybody calls me Pree. Mum's a horse breeder. She breeds Arabians. That's how I got so much practice at mucking out. I'm not allowed to touch her horses, but. They're worth too much money. I have my own pony called Jasmine. She's so fat I can hardly get a girth round her. If I don't put her on a serious diet and exercise program, I'll end up riding everywhere bareback.'

I stared at her, wondering where the off switch was. I'd never met anyone who talked so much, ever! I was surprised she hadn't fainted from lack of oxygen.

'Pree, Pree—'

Pree laughed. 'How'd you know Mum calls me that? She's got a whole heap of names for me.' Pree began counting off on her fingers. 'There's Pree-Pree, Preepers, Preencess, Pree-Diddles—'

'Whoa!' I held up my hands. Pree stopped, mid-word. Her mouth hung open, like I'd pressed 'pause'. For a second.

'Preezy-Boo—'

'Wait! Did you just say "Preezy-Boo"?'

'It gets worse. When I started school I only answered to Preety-Bops.' Pree giggled then and it was all so weird I had to join in. By the time we'd finished mucking out the stalls I knew Pree had a two-year-old brother called Raji (who had ripped her favourite unicorn bookmark to shreds just the night before — Pree's advice: lock your room) and that she'd been dying to start work at Shady Trails because, according to Pree, no amount of poo shovelling could ever be as bad as having to go to her mum's Indian dance class. It wasn't the dancing that was the problem, it was the tripping on the hem of your sari.

'I've got two left RM Williams,' she explained. 'Just like Dad. That's how they met. He needed to learn a dance for his brother's wedding and she was the teacher. It was love at first Bhangra — that's an Indian dance.'

'Wow!' I said, wide-eyed. 'So where're you from?'

Pree tossed her plait over her shoulder. 'Pinebark Ridge.'

I shook my head. 'No, what part of India are you from?'

Pree stared at me, blankly. 'Pinebark Ridge. Dad's parents were born in Agra, near the Taj Mahal. But

Mum's mum's dad's great-grandfather came out on the Second Fleet. He was a horse-stealer from somewhere in Scotland. Mum reckons that's how she got into the business.'

'But the Indian dancing?' I was so confused.

Pree giggled. 'It's funny, eh? But that's my mum. She got into it as a kid and got so good she started her own dance school. Now she just teaches on Saturday.'

I looked at the clock on the wall. Muck-outs were done. It was time for pony round-ups.

I grabbed some lead ropes from the hook on the wall, looped them over my shoulder and tucked three carrots from Honey's secret stash into my shirt pocket. She was out grazing and making friends so I figured she wouldn't mind.

'Are we catching the horses?' Pree asked, following me out of the stables and to the day paddock where the ponies were kept. 'Can I catch one? Which horses are they? Are we going to tack them up? Where are they? Do you wanna hear a joke?'

I wiggled my finger in my ear. I'd heard of industrial deafness before but this was ridiculous. 'I—'

'How do cows keep in touch with each other?' Pree skipped along beside me, her plait bouncing on her back.

'Um—'

'With moobile phones! D'you get it? Moobile phones!'

Pree cracked up laughing. I smiled despite myself.

Bartok, Brandy and Paris were grazing together in the corner of the day paddock. I called out to them and they looked up at once. Bartok stretched out his head and whinnied. He hadn't known me long, but long enough to know I meant treats.

Bartok took a few steps towards us. I pulled out the carrots and held them up. That was enough for Bartok. He trotted over to me and nuzzled my hand. I fed him a carrot and clipped the lead rope onto his headstall. I passed the end of the rope to Pree. She kissed Bartok on the nose and began telling him all about Raji's second birthday party where they'd had a horse piñata and it wouldn't break, so her dad chopped its head off with an axe and all the kids screamed and cried.

Leaving Pree and Bartok to get to know one another, I set off after Brandy and Paris. They hadn't budged but were watching me, waiting to see what I'd do next.

Brandy tossed his head. He seemed to be saying, 'Ha-ha, made you walk all the way over here!'

'Cheeky!' I scolded. 'You really don't deserve this carrot.'

I fastened the lead rope to his headstall and he rubbed his head on my shoulder. 'How can I resist you now?'

I gave him his carrot and Paris's ears twitched at the sound of Brandy's happy munching. She stretched out her head, her nostrils quivering.

'Gotcha!' I said, clipping on the last lead rope. Paris was rewarded with her carrot and I led the two crunching ponies back to Pree and Bartok.

Two girls and a boy who had come to the grand opening were coming in for a group riding lesson. They were all beginners and the ponies were ideal for them to learn on.

Pree and I tacked them up quickly, saddle first of course, and gave their forelegs a good stretch (I had to hand it to Pree, she could talk underwater with a mouth full of marbles, but she knew horses). Then we led them to the holding yard and secured them to the fence with loops of twine, which would break more easily than rope or reins if they spooked.

'What's next?' Pree said. 'I love working with horses. I'll do anything. Just name it. Just tell me and I'll do it. No probs. No questions asked. Just as long as it's something to do with horses and I'll—'

'Pree!' I was exasperated.

'Yeah?' Pree was giving me a footy-stadium-floodlight smile.

I took a deep breath, relieved that Sam had arrived in the holding yard with the three little kids.

'Gidday, Ash, Preezy!' Sam gave us a wink and hoisted each kid into the saddle. After five minutes of stirrup, girth and chin-strap adjusting, Sam led them off to their lesson, the kids giggling and squealing in delight. I could definitely relate to that. A big part of me wished to be back there again — to a time when riding was new and a whole wondrous world was opening up to me for the first time.

'What do we do now, Ash?' Pree's voice ripped me out of my daydream.

'I'll give you the tour. Then we'll check and clean today's tack and fill the haynets in the stalls.'

Pree was delirious. 'Sounds great! Wanna hear

another joke? What do you call a donkey with three legs? A wonky! D'you get it? A wonky!'

Pree fell apart laughing and this time I joined in. It felt so good to laugh with her after all the stress with Becky over Shady Trails.

I stuck out my hand and we shook for the second time that day, still giggling, my cheeks aching. 'Pree, I think this is the beginning of a pretty awesome mateship!'

Pree's mum (who drove a really cool four-wheel drive with stickers on the back window that said *Poverty is owning a horse* and *Love is an Arab*) came to pick her up at the end of the day. Honey was tacked up and ready to go, but there was something eating at me. I scratched, but it wasn't fleas. It was fear. Chewing at my heart and tingling all the way down to my toes.

I couldn't deliver the brochures, I just couldn't. All day it had been in the back of my mind and no amount of Pree's jokes had made it go away. Becky had been hurt enough by my decision to work at Shady Trails. I could imagine how upset she'd be if she saw me with the brochures, let alone if she saw me on them!

I left Honey with Azz, who set about checking her legs and feet (as he said, leg checks for horses had to be as much a part of any horse's daily routine as brushing our teeth is for us humans) and made my way to Mrs McMurray's office. I'd never actually been inside her office before but I knew where to find it. As I got closer I could hear loud music, classical music, playing. I wrinkled my nose. I'd never been all that 'into' the classics. The William Tell Overture was about the closest I'd ever come to classical music and only because it was a great piece to gallop around the lounge room to while wearing a home-made horsetail pinned to the seat of your pants and making clopping hoof sounds with your tongue. I'd won many a Melbourne Cup to that piece.

I knocked on the office door and the music was turned down a little.

'Come in.'

I opened the door and took a step inside. The room was neat, clean and smelled of new carpet. Mrs McMurray was sitting behind her desk typing something on the computer, her glasses resting on the tip of her nose. I'd never seen her with glasses, but she looked nice in them.

'What's up, Ash?'

'I ... um ...' I realised then that I didn't know what to say. I felt like I was in the principal's office and that I'd done something really bad. My guts wriggled like I'd swallowed a bucketful of worms.

'Yes?' Mrs McMurray watched me. I writhed under her scrutiny. I was suddenly conscious of my muddy boots and grass-stained joddies. Actually, there were mud stains on them as well. Plus horsehair, sawdust, a streak of manure and carroty horse dribble. I smoothed down my hair, hoping that a dazzling hairdo would make every other imperfection seem as meaningless as a book with not one single horse in it. But with that music playing, I felt for the first time that I really didn't belong at Shady Trails.

'Is everything all right, love?' Mrs McMurray said.

I nodded quickly. 'Yeah. No problems. I just wanted to, ah, tell you I'm going home.'

'Had a good day?' Mrs McMurray turned the music down a little more. I was getting kind of used to it, though, and was sure I could hear something like a trumpet playing.

'I had a great day!' I gushed. 'It's so great here. Really great.'

Mrs McMurray gestured to the chair right in front of her desk. 'Do you want to sit down, love?'

I sat quickly. 'Thanks.'

Mrs McMurray leaned towards me, her elbows on the desk. 'How did you like Priyanka?'

I nodded again. 'She knows a lot about horses.'

'Doctor Prasad is my GP. Apparently she told him joke after joke until he promised to call me and ask if there was a job here for her. I was only too happy to end his suffering.' Mrs McMurray smiled. Her blue eyes were gentle and warm.

I laughed. 'Sounds like Pree.'

Was there a good time or a good way to tell her that I couldn't possibly do as she'd asked me?

'What's the matter, Ash? Looks like you're not enjoying my CD.'

'No, it's just ... I don't know a lot about classical music.' I was squirming.

'What kind of music do you like?'

I bit my bottom lip the way I always do when I'm stressed. 'Um, I, modern stuff, mainly. Anything I can dance to.'

Mrs McMurray smiled. 'Close your eyes, love.'

I hesitated, biting down harder.

'Close them,' she said softly. I obeyed. The music ran over me like sweet rain. 'Now, imagine the most spectacular, the most exquisite Lipizzaner stallions. Their coats are white and sleek. They're performing the Quadrille, dancing in perfect unison to this beautiful music. Can you see them?'

I could. I really could! I nodded, breathless.

'Now what do you think?'

I opened my eyes. 'What's this song called?'

Mrs McMurray smiled again. 'The Brandenburg Concerto, Number Two.'

I grinned at her. 'It's not so bad.'

'Not bad at all,' Mrs McMurray said, smiling back at me. She tucked her silver hair behind her ears.

I felt bold all of a sudden. 'Why do you like this music so much?'

Mrs McMurray sighed and leaned back into her chair. 'It's such a long story, Ash.'

My heart jumped in my chest. 'Sorry, I shouldn't have—'

Mrs McMurray held up her hand. 'No, it's okay.' She sighed again and took off her glasses, rubbing each lens slowly on her shirt. She squinted into them and replaced her glasses carefully. 'My husband was a cellist. He would go into the sunroom to play every night after dinner. I would wash up then make myself a coffee, sit with him and listen to his music. It's too quiet here after dinner.'

'You should come to my place some time. It's never quiet. Not any more.'

Mrs McMurray raised her eyebrows and before I knew what was happening I was telling her all about Jason and how Mum was always tired and sad. I told her how the baby wouldn't sleep and how he cried all the time and how we only ever had takeaway dinners. I told her that Mum and Dad hardly noticed me, and probably wouldn't even if I wore a nappy on my head and did the chicken dance. I realised then I was crying and for a moment I was ashamed. But Mrs McMurray reached out her hand and patted mine, horse grime and all.

By the time I left her office, her brochures tucked safely in my saddlebag, I felt better than I had since the day I'd become a big sister. I would deliver the brochures — I owed her that. I owed Becky, too, I knew it. I also knew I had to figure out a way to make them both happy, without hurting either one in the process.

Nine

Trails of Treachery

'I know just what to do,' Becky said. I'd invited her over to watch DVDs in my room. We were lying on our tummies side by side on my bed and less than five minutes into *Mounted Games for Riding Clubs* when she was struck by her brilliant idea.

'What?' I mumbled through a mouthful of prawn chips. They're one of my favourites, which Becky knows. She always brings me a bag or two from the restaurant, but never eats any! Every time I offer her some she just shakes her head muttering how over them she is and waves them away.

Becky rolled her eyes. 'I dunno how you can eat

those things. In fact, I dunno how you can eat anything in that position.'

'Rebecca, my dearest friend, I can eat anything, anyhow.'

Becky covered her ears with her hands. 'Please tell me I didn't just hear you call me Rebecca.' She said her own name like it was a particularly unpleasant equine fungus.

'I didn't just call you Rebecca.' I giggled, unable to resist, and crunched on another prawn chip. I slapped my foot against hers, trying to tempt her into a toe-wrestle.

'Ash, this is serious!' Becky sat up straight on the bed and whacked me with a pillow. Prawn chips flew across the room like tiny UFOs.

I snatched the pillow and shoved it under my tummy, grinning at her with soggy bits stuck between my teeth then dug around in the bag and squeezed a whole chip into my mouth in one go.

'I'm gonna make brochures, you know, to advertise Riding Club. We have to get membership up,' Becky said, lying next to me again.

'We?' I stopped chewing. My mouth was full of half-eaten prawn chip.

Becky laughed. 'Of course "we". Whaddya reckon? We're best friends, aren't we?'

I nodded, trying to swallow down what felt like a wad of newspaper in my mouth. I didn't know what to say. I'd already delivered most of the Shady Trails brochures. I only had a few left, which I was hiding in my desk and had promised to give out at the gymkhana.

Somehow when Becky wasn't looking, of course.

'Speaking of brochures, did you know some clown has been handing out Shady Trails brochures all over Shady Creek?'

I shrugged.

'Unbelievable, eh? I tell you, if I ever catch them I'll make 'em eat every last one.' Becky laughed then. I was too horrified to do anything but stare at her. 'If I could get my hands on those brochures I'd use them to line the budgie's cage. That'll show the traitor.'

'Let's watch the DVD,' I said, poking Becky in the ribs, my heart beating so loudly I was sure Becky would ask me to turn it down. 'We need as many tips as we can get before Saturday. Are we still cutting a cake for you at lunch?'

The gymkhana (and Becky's birthday) was only days away and aside from the fact I'd found her the most ace present, I'd never felt more unprepared. Becky, the twins and I had trained as much as we could after school, but I had the feeling it wasn't going to be enough. Flea's hysterical reaction to every move we made hadn't helped. And seeing him fall backwards off the fence that separated my place from his and land in Scud's water trough hadn't been as delicious for any of us as it normally would have been.

'A cake?' Becky said absentmindedly, as though turning twelve was the least important thing in the world to her. I don't know about you, but I hang out for my birthday. It's the best day of the year. Worst part is it takes a whole year to have another one.

'Yeah, we'll do that.' Becky sat bolt upright. I could practically see the light bulb switch on over her dark head. 'You're the Empress of Ideas! What else d'you reckon we can do? We organised all that fundraising before for the Cross-Country Championships so we shouldn't do anything like that. We need something new and fresh!'

I felt sick all of a sudden. It could have been the one and a half bags of prawn chips I'd chowed my way through. But it was more likely the thought of what I'd been doing behind Becky's back.

'C'mon, Beck. Let's just watch the DVD, okay?' I said, clutching my stomach. 'We can talk about this—'

'There's no time to waste!' Becky jumped off my bed and pulled on her shoes. 'We need paper and pens. We can make a list and start working on a brochure. We should do it in black felt pen on white paper. That way I can ask Mrs Jacobs to run it off for us on the photocopier at school. I know!'

Becky's face changed. She went from looking like someone who was really excited about having a good idea to someone who looked like they'd just come up with something so dazzling it was enough to knock the socks off Einstein himself. Her light bulb had grown into a floodlight.

'We can give them out at the gymkhana!'

I coughed, thinking about the brochures in my desk drawer and how I'd promised Mrs McMurray, and Becky's birthday and my gymkhana team. I thought about Gary and Honey and Charlie, and I even thought about the Creepketeers. What if Shady Creek Riding Club really did close? Would Flea, Carly and Ryan find a new riding school for themselves at Shady Trails? I couldn't bear to think about it.

'Ashleigh, what's this?'

I zapped back to reality. Becky was standing by my desk. The drawer was open and she was holding a coloured paper in her hand. It was glossy and had a familiar picture in the bottom right-hand corner of a kid with two light brown pigtails and a grin so wide you could park your bike in it.

Becky took a long look at the paper. Then she looked at me. I'd never seen her look so shocked. 'It was you? You're the traitor?'

I shrank back into the bed. 'Becky, I—'

'No, Ash! There's nothing you can say. Nothing can change this!' Becky's face was red. Her eyes were narrow and her lips were thin. I'd never seen her so angry, ever.

I rubbed my forehead with my hands and sat up. If I had to fight with Becky I didn't want to be face-down when it happened. 'Just let me—'

'Let you what?' Becky said. She was holding the brochure so tightly it was crumpling in her grip.

I stood up. 'Let me explain.'

Becky took a step backwards. 'There's nothing to explain. You've made your decision — that much is obvious.'

I was so scared, so horrified. This wasn't what I wanted. I had known that Becky would be upset, but nothing like this. 'Becky, why can't you—'

'Don't talk to me, Ashleigh. Just open your eyes for once. Can't you see that Riding Club is going under?' Becky's eyes were brimming with tears.

I wished I could take it all back, that I could reverse the clock and take it all back.

'Don't you have any idea how hard Dad's worked? He's given everything to Riding Club and never asked for anything and this is how you repay him?'

I reached my hand out towards her but she took step after step away from me, like she couldn't get out of my sight fast enough. 'Becky, please.' I was crying now. It wasn't worth this. Nothing was worth this.

'You see this, Ashleigh?' Becky held up the Shady Trails brochure. She tore it in half and scrunched up the pieces, throwing them to the floor. 'This is what you can do with Shady Trails.'

Standing there, watching Becky tear up the brochure with my face on it, I knew what Becky had been trying to tell me for weeks. I just hadn't been listening.

'This isn't about your dad, is it? Not all of it.' I wiped at my nose with the back of my hand. I must have looked a mess but I didn't care.

Becky coughed. She was crying. She stared up at the ceiling for a moment and I knew it was because she just couldn't speak. She took a deep breath. 'Riding Club is all I ever had in Shady Creek. Then you came and I had you and Riding Club and it was so perfect. But now that Shady Trails woman is taking everything away from me and you're helping her, Ashleigh. You're actually helping her and that's what hurts the most.'

'What are you saying?'

Becky held up her chin and looked me in the eye. She'd stopped crying. She was wearing the same face she wore on the first day I'd ever met her. A mask that protected her from all the hurt that came with being Rebecca Cho in Shady Creek. 'Choose, Ash. Right here, right now: it's me or Shady Trails.'

'But I need this job. I need to keep Horse Cents

going!' It was true. With Mum at home with Jason and Dad working minimum hours to come home and help, Shady Trails was Honey's only chance of hay and horseshoes.

Becky refused to look at me. She picked up her helmet from my desk and stepped out of my room. When she finally spoke it was in a voice I didn't recognise. 'You made the choice, Ashleigh, not me. I thought we were best friends. I was wrong.'

Becky turned and ran downstairs. I stared after her, weak with shock. It wasn't long before I heard Charlie's hooves beating down the driveway and I wondered if I'd ever hear them again.

I curled up on my bed, staring at the two crumpled-up pieces of brochure on the floor and sobbed. This was the first time in my life when I'd felt real pain, pain so big I could feel it in every bone, in every fibre of my body. I wanted Becky back, I wanted Jenna, I wanted my mum.

When I couldn't cry any more I went looking for my parents. My legs felt like two bags of wet chaff. My head pounded and I felt sick. But all of that was nothing compared to the pain in my chest. So this is what it is, I thought, to have a broken heart.

I found them in Jason's room, fussing like possums.

'I need . . .' I said. It was more like wheezing than speaking. I couldn't get the words out.

'Haven't cooked any dinner, Ash,' Mum said, not even looking up. 'Jason's been going nuts all afternoon.'

Dad patted my head. 'Why don't you go make a sandwich and we'll get takeaway later on? How does Rebecca's Garden grab you?'

The room started spinning. I sucked in air but couldn't seem to get enough. Why didn't they realise? Why couldn't they see me any more? I pointed at Jason and screamed louder than I ever had in my life.

'I hate him. I hate him and I hate you! Are you listening to me now? I hate all of you!'

For the first time in my life I made my mother cry. Jason joined in. Good, I thought. Now maybe they'll feel what I'm feeling. Now maybe they'll understand. Dad gave me a look that would give a cockroach a coronary.

'Get out of this room, Miss. And don't come back until you're ready to apologise and if that means you starve, then you starve.'

'Good!' I shrieked. I slammed Jason's door and ran downstairs, across the driveway and into Honey's paddock. I found her under her favourite tree and threw my arms around her neck crying harder than I ever had before. I had to get out of there. I scrambled onto Honey's bare back and used her mane to neck-rein her to her stable. I tacked her up quickly, tears spilling down my face, mounted and cantered down the driveway. I didn't care where we went — I let Honey make the decisions. All I knew was that I had to ride her, I had to feel that with every step she took, the pounding of her hooves took away a tiny piece of my pain. We rode and rode and rode and by the time we pulled up outside Shady Trails Riding Ranch, I felt better.

Ten

Gymkhana Blues

The alarm rang and rang. I lay still in my bed, hiding under the doona, trying to pretend that it wasn't Saturday morning. Gymkhana day. Becky's twelfth birthday.

I heard footsteps, then my door flew open. I peeked out from under the covers. Mum was standing in the middle of my room in her pyjamas. Her hair and eyes were wild, like a tropical cyclone had swept her up and dropped her through the roof. She panted for a few moments, then marched towards my alarm clock, grabbed it by the cord and yanked so hard the plug was ripped from the wall.

I flipped the doona over my head, but it was quickly ripped off.

'What's wrong with you, Ashleigh?' Mum hissed, in what can only be described as a scrisper — the scream you do when you're trying to whisper. 'Jason kept me up all night. He's finally asleep and the last thing I want is you waking him up just as I'm getting to bed.'

I shrugged and rolled over.

It had been two days since my fight with Becky and, even though I'd apologised to Mum and Dad, they still hadn't noticed that I'd been hanging around the house on my own or riding Honey by myself and hadn't phoned my best friend even once.

'Now that you've woken up the whole house you may as well get out of bed and get ready for school.' Mum smoothed down her hair a little.

I shook my head. Now that I had lost my best friend I didn't want to do anything. I didn't want to get up. I didn't want to get dressed. I didn't want to eat or drink or smile. And for the first time in my life I didn't want to go to a gymkhana. All I wanted was to have Becky back and the chances of that were about as slim as my chances of posting Jason on eBay.

Mum wrenched open my wardrobe and scooped up my school uniform from the floor. She tossed it at me and slammed the wardrobe shut again. 'Get ready for school. You might want to take your jacket — it's blowing a gale out there.'

I rolled onto my tummy and mumbled into my pillow. 'It's Saturday.'

Mum frowned and looked at the alarm clock. It had nothing to say. 'So I guess you'll be going to work today? Or maybe going to Becky's?' She sounded hopeful. She sounded normal, actually, and hadn't cried for a whole day.

I groaned and punched my pillow. 'It's gymkhana day. I've been talking about it for weeks, Mum. Remember I asked you guys to come?'

Mum sighed and closed her eyes. 'I can't, possum. Not today.'

I wasn't surprised but I was mad. 'But why? I asked you after my first day back at Riding Club and you said okay.'

Mum pushed me out of bed and tugged at my sheet. 'That was before.'

I stood opposite her with my hands on my hips

and my hair looking like I was a breeding house for static electricity. 'Before what?'

Mum pulled my doona up over the sheet and smoothed down the bed. She hadn't made my bed since Year Four. 'Before Jason, Ash. He's too little to go to a gymkhana. It's getting colder. I'll need to feed and change him. And look how windy it is.' Mum reached across the bed and squeezed my hand. 'I forgot what it was like to have a small baby, Ash. Try to understand.'

I snatched my hand away. Why was it always me who had to understand?

I sat down on the bed with my back to my mother. 'Don't bother. I'll be fine on my own.'

'Oh, Ash,' Mum said.

She laid her hands on my shoulders and I shook them off. I felt mean. But I was hurt, and I'd been on the planet long enough to know that people can sometimes be mean when their feelings have been trampled by a herd of mountain brumbies.

By the time Honey and I arrived at the Shady Creek and Districts Showground I had enough mud on my joddies to build my own mountain,

Honey's tail was full of windblown leaves and I'd lost my dark blue club ribbon. Hoping that these misfortunes were good luck rather than particularly bad omens, I dismounted and led my Honey horse through the mass of saddled horses, kids in Riding Club outfits and anxious parents weighed down by armloads of tack, riding jackets and Eskies. I was relieved that Julie and Jodie had come to the rescue and agreed to cart all my gear over in their double float.

Honey and I were looking for the Shady Creek Riding Club camp. Usually I would have hitched a ride with Becky and known precisely where it was. But there was no way I could have endured the ten-minute car ride in total silence, staring out of the window and sitting as far away from Becky as I possibly could.

After a while I spotted a familiar dark blue and gold club banner flapping about and made a beeline for it. The usual clubs were there. Pinebark Ridge in their green shirts had set up camp under a huge tree, which was bending and swaying. I led Honey past them eyeing them up and down.

'Ash? Is that you?'

A girl with a brilliant pair of white teeth jumped out of the Pinebark Ridge contingent.

'Pree!' I was confused and excited to see her all at once. 'What're you doing here?'

Pree grabbed my hands. 'It's you! It's really you. This is so cool. I never knew you were a Riding Clubber. Hey, you guys!'

Pinebark Ridge turned and stared. I shrank as Pree introduced me. It felt strange being so close to so many green shirts. I'd never liked anyone from Pinebark Ridge, but never met any of them either. They all seemed human enough — maybe even nice.

'Shady Creek's over there,' Pree said, pointing at the banner. 'I just have to warn you, though.' Pree lowered her voice to the best whisper she could manage. 'I shouldn't really be talking to you here. Ridgers don't really like Creekers all that much. But you're different.'

I smiled. 'Thanks, Pree.'

Pree turned her attention to Honey. 'Hi beautiful! She's so gorgeous. How old is she? How many hands did you say she was? Are you sure she's not a Thoroughbred? She looks like she has some racing blood in her. Maybe even quarter horse. How long've you had her, again? How d'you reckon she'll go in this weather? Have you heard this one? Why are horses hopeless dancers? Coz they have two left feet!'

'Spiller!' shrieked a voice. There was no blue ribbon for guessing whose it was.

I rolled my eyes. 'Pree, I have to go.'

Pree beamed and told me she'd see me later.

''Bout time you turned up,' Carly said as I led Honey into the Shady Creek Riding Club camp. Becky was grooming Charlie by her float. She must have heard Carly announcing my arrival but she didn't even look up. I scanned the camp quickly for the twins but couldn't see them or their ponies.

'Nice of you to grace us with your presence.' Carly had a look of smug superiority on her pale face. Flea and Ryan stood behind her with their arms folded.

'Give it a rest,' I said. 'Nobody here is interested.'

'Oooohhh.' Carly nudged Flea. 'Thinks she's tough.'

'I don't, actually,' I said. 'But I do think you're an idiot.'

I stroked Honey's neck and led her to the fence, leaving Carly staring after me. In true Carly style, it didn't take her too long to recover.

'You can't talk to me like that, Spiller.'

'Why not?' I threw the words over my shoulder into the wind, concentrating on my Honey horse and refusing to even look at Carly. I knew that if I did meet her eyes she'd see instantly how terrified I was. Three against two was bad enough. Three against one was impossible.

Carly bounded over, followed by her permanent shadows, her hair pulled back so tight into its regulation red riding bun I was sure she'd eventually go bald. She poked my back. Her finger felt like a knitting needle.

'Coz you don't belong here. You never have. The sooner you get that through your fat head the better.'

I loosened Honey's girth and shortened my stirrups. 'Sticks and stones, Carly. Sticks and stones.'

I said it, but I didn't mean it. I felt the pain from Carly's words. Pushing the feelings as deep as I could, I got on with the job at hand. I unbuckled the noseband then the throatlash of Honey's bridle and slipped the headpiece over her ears. Laying the reins over my left arm (and, just in case Honey spooked and bolted, making sure I hadn't looped them around my arm), I moved the bridle gently down her face, letting her release the bit from her mouth on her own. Once the bridle was free of Honey's head and secured on my arm with the reins, I slipped her headstall on and tied her lead rope to the fence through a loop of twine.

'Where's your little Garden friend?' Carly said 'friend' as though the word could choke her. She hadn't yet tired of her game. 'Why hasn't she come to your rescue?'

I shrugged. 'Why don't you go see for yourself?'

It was then that she clued in. The nasty sneer she'd worn since she'd begun her attack was replaced with a look of such unadulterated joy it made me sick.

'Could it be?' Carly gasped. 'The greatest friendship of all time is over?' She threw her head back and laughed. 'Oh, this is the best, I'm gonna have so much fun!'

Operation Creep began. Flea, Carly and Ryan surrounded me. Step by step, closer and closer.

'Spiller, Spiller, Spiller,' they chanted. 'Spiller, Spiller.'

They were so close I could feel the warmth of their bodies on the bare skin of my arms. The hairs on the back of my neck prickled. Fear rose as a huge lump in my throat.

I didn't know where to go or what to do. I could run away, but I'd never leave Honey with them, not for anything. I could scream for help, but then they'd know how much they were scaring me. Or I could stay with Honey and wait for it to be over.

I slipped my arms around Honey's neck and hugged her close. Nothing could hurt me when I was with her. We'd made a promise, a sacred promise, that we'd never leave each other. She knew I would always be there for her and I knew likewise. The wind shook us but I clung to her, closed my eyes and breathed her in. I felt her breathing and the Creeps' chant dimmed a little.

'Ash? Ash, what's going on?'

I thought I'd heard someone speaking but I wasn't sure. I kept my eyes closed, my arms around Honey. It was safer this way.

'Ashleigh!'

It was then I noticed the chant had stopped. I opened my eyes and blinked up at Gary. He looked down at me, confused.

'Is everything okay? Becky said you wanted to ride Honey over yourself today, warm her up some.'

I nodded. There was no way I could have said anything to him without crying. Becky had lied to Gary about me. My whole body stung.

Gary smiled and patted my shoulder. 'We're just about to have a quick club meeting, so when you're ready?'

I nodded again, but couldn't look at him. It just hurt so much. She'd lied to him. She hadn't even looked at me. She'd let me be terrorised by the Creepketeers when we had vowed to stick together no matter what. All over a bunch of dumb brochures!

I joined the meeting but didn't really hear a word Gary said. Every now and then I looked at Becky. She was wearing it again — that mask.

I felt a tap on my shoulder. Julie and Jodie had arrived at last. I was so relieved I could have kissed them both.

'What's up?' Jodie asked, grinning at me.

I shook my head. 'Heaps. I'm just glad you're here.'

Julie frowned. 'What happened?'

I sighed. 'Nothing I can't handle.'

'I saw Honey — she looks great!'

I'd been up since before sunrise grooming Honey, polishing her tack and braiding her mane and tail. I had a few tricks up my sleeve when it came to horse beauty. Like sticking down wispy bits of mane with hair gel and doing lots of plaits for a shorter neck or fewer plaits for a longer neck. I knew to plait the forelock with the hair strands crossed under instead of over to make the plait stand out and to wipe Honey's muzzle with baby oil (there was plenty of that at home!) to make it look clean and shiny. I knew to rub white chalk into Honey's socks and the long white blaze on her face to make them stand out and to trim the hair around her ears, fetlocks and under her chin. I knew to carefully pick every last leaf, twig and prickle from her tail before entering the arena. I knew all those things, but I didn't know how to fix things with my best friend.

Honey was bridled and ready to go. It was our first event, the individual showjumping, and I was so full of nerves I had my teeth clamped shut to stop those nerves bursting out of my mouth. I'd been waiting for this chance for weeks and my stay at Waratah Grove had only made me more determined. I was going to show the Shady Creek riders exactly what Honey and I could do.

Honey was warmed up, my stirrups were shortened two notches, I'd walked the course and at least two people in the stands (Julie and Jodie) had their fingers crossed for me. We were as ready as we could hope to be.

I sat mounted on Honey in the marshalling area, my number strapped over my new black body protector (I'd finally bought my own with some of my Waratah Grove prize money). I was as far away from Becky as I could be. It wasn't that I didn't want to be near her. It was just that I was sure she didn't want to be anywhere near me. Having to share the small marshalling area with Carly wasn't any fun either. Apparently convinced that occasionally hissing my dreaded nickname would freak me out and help her win, she devoted the first five minutes of the event to doing exactly that. Until a large girl in a purple Jacaranda Tops Riding Club shirt, and mounted on what looked like a cross between a

Percheron and a Clydesdale, informed Carly that if she didn't stop making 'that snake sound' she'd soon be picking her own helmet out of her teeth.

The riders were called one by one. Pree wasn't riding for Pinebark Ridge, but I recognised a boy called Joey who'd tried out for the Waratah Grove Junior Cross-Country Riding Championships last summer.

Becky was called at last.

'Good lu—' I stopped myself before the rest of the word came out. Becky seemed to look back for a moment, then rode out into Ring Two. I watched her take Charlie over the jumps, one by one. She jumped him perfectly. Their run was clean, no mistakes, no penalties. But something was missing. There was no sparkle. It was almost like she didn't love it any more.

'Ashleigh Miller.'

I gathered my reins and squeezed Honey's sides, grateful to Clydesdale Girl who'd only had to point to Carly's helmet and bare her teeth to make Carly think better of sending me off with another rendition of the 'Spiller Chant'.

I wanted to do well. I had to do well. I was determined — I might not have a best friend any more but that didn't mean I wasn't going to give everything I had for my horse and my club.

We entered the ring. Honey trotted smoothly beneath me. I rose and sat again in time with her strides for half the length of the ring then urged her into a canter by closing my legs in on her ribcage, just behind her girth. We had thirty seconds left to begin the course. I wheeled her round to face the first jump.

'Just like at the Grove,' I murmured to her. 'Just like we did at the Grove.'

We cantered towards the jump, a single oxer suspended between two huge white wings. Honey had jumped these more times than she'd had hot bran mashes, but that didn't stop me from worrying. What if she clipped a rail or, worse, brought it crashing down? What if she refused a jump? The wind whipped at us. What if it whipped a plastic bag into the ring and spooked her totally? The possibilities for disaster were endless.

We cantered on. When she was about three strides away I sat down in the saddle, leaned forward and used my legs behind her girth, holding my reins short and my hands low.

Honey lowered her head and stretched her neck, then sprang upwards, stretching out long and tucking her forelegs under her chest and her hind legs under her belly. We sailed over the jump, the wind beating so hard against us if I'd been riding any other horse we'd have been blown away. But my Honey stayed strong, focussed. She reached out with her forelegs and shortened her neck, bringing her head up as her feet touched down. The first jump was clear. Only eleven to go!

Eleven

Bad Eggs

'Awesome, Ash!' Julie said, holding up my red second-place ribbon. We were leaning against a tree, giving the horses a rest in the shade. The wind had died down a little, but still had a sting.

'Totally awesome!' Jodie offered me an apple. I accepted it and took a huge bite. It was crunchy and juicy together. I'd been too anxious to eat anything all day, but now I had one ribbon under my belt I felt better. Almost well enough to be nervous enough to need something to eat!

'Blue is a much better colour on me,' I said with a wink. 'But I'm happy with red.'

Jodie hid a huge smile behind her apple. 'Better

than Carly's efforts. She's as green as the ribbon on that Pinebark Ridge boy's horse.'

I had to smile as well. Carly was probably being forced to change her strategy from 'If you freak Ash, she will lose' to 'If I spent as much time preparing for my event as I do trying to make Ashleigh drop her bundle maybe I have a chance at a ribbon'.

'Is Becky doing the dressage with you?' Julie said, smiling.

I nodded stiffly, flicking a piece of green apple skin into the dirt. 'Last I heard.'

An announcer's voice began crackling out of the loudspeaker nearby. Junior dressage was being called to Ring Two. I scrambled to my feet and made a dash to Julie and Jodie's float, which was also serving as our change room, tack shed, feed bin and rest station. The twins' mum, Mrs Ferguson, was horsy enough to know that a well-placed mattress never goes astray at an all-day gymkhana. So far each of us had flopped down for a mini siesta.

I emerged from the float changed into my new dressage outfit. I'd gone on a shopping spree at Planet Horse in town and bought not only my shiny new body protector but a new pair of black chaps, a black jacket, a white collared shirt with long, button-up sleeves, cream gloves and a bright blue tie with cream spots. For the first time at a gymkhana I looked like a real rider.

'You look cool, Ash,' Julie said.

'Cool!' Jodie walked around me a few times. 'Price tag!' She giggled and snapped the rectangular piece of cardboard from my sleeve just before she and Julie were hustled away by Mrs Ferguson to pay a visit to the little fillies' room. I remembered something suddenly and patted my jacket pocket, sighing with relief. It was still there.

'Ashleigh!'

I spun around. Becky, also dressed in her best riding clothes, was being dragged towards me by her mother. She looked amazing. But then, she always did.

'Hi, sweetie,' Mrs Cho said. She looked flustered. 'I've been looking for you everywhere.'

She shoved Becky at me and took out her camera. I don't know what was more shocking — standing so close to Becky or seeing Mrs Cho at a gymkhana. She's about as horsy as Jenna and usually does her best to find something urgent to do on gymkhana days, like polishing doorknobs. 'I promised your mum a photo.'

I stood beside my ex-best friend and stared at the camera. Becky did likewise.

Mrs Cho frowned at her screen. 'What is it with everyone today? Smile, girls, smile!'

I did my best to force my lips into a curl but I must have looked like I was having cramps because Mrs Cho frowned even harder.

'No, no, that's no good. A real smile. Becky, tell one of your jokes. Ash, put your arm around Becky.'

I froze.

'Ash,' Mrs Cho said again. 'Your arm — put it around Becky. Huddle up and smile.'

I looked at Becky and for the first time that day, she looked at me. We both knew what neither wanted to say out loud. We would have to play along — for the time being anyway.

I put my arm around Becky's shoulders. Becky edged a little closer to me. We showed our teeth for the photo and, as soon as it was taken and Mrs Cho dashed away again, jumped apart as though we were afraid of catching something.

It was just the two of us, then. I didn't know what to do, so I started talking.

'I'm sorry — about the brochures.'

Becky looked away. 'I don't want to talk about it.'

'We need to talk about it. We have to talk about it.'

'There's nothing to say.' Becky looked at her gloves.

I wanted to scream. 'There's plenty to say. I've already said I'm sorry. Can't you just get over it?'

Becky regarded me through narrow eyes. 'I'm getting Charlie.'

I grabbed her arm. She looked at my hand like it was a piece of rubbish whipped up by the wind. 'Please stop this. We can get through anything. We promised each other we'd always stick together. Becky, we're best friends!'

Becky looked at me with cold eyes. She looked unfamiliar. It was like someone I didn't know was staring back at me. 'Correction. We *were* best friends.'

I let my hand slip from Becky's arm and she walked away, her head held high, her long black plait shining against her back. My chest squeezed and tears welled up in my eyes.

Two hands covered my eyes from behind. 'Guess who?'

I shrugged.

Pree jumped out in front of me. 'It's me! Are you riding dressage? How unreal. I've never ridden dressage. I like barrel racing best. You know what I always say? Barrel racing is life, the rest is just details. Ash? Ash, what's wrong?'

I wiped at the tears that had started rolling down my face one after the other and took a deep, shaky breath. 'It's . . . it's just that my old instructor used to say that and I miss her.'

Pree looked at me, her eyes wide with concern. 'Are you sure that's it?'

I nodded and hooked my arm through hers. 'Wanna be my cheer squad?'

Pree beamed. Her teeth were truly dazzling. 'You betcha.'

It felt good to be with her and even better when, from the marshalling area of Ring Two, I could see her in the stands waving at me.

I was nervous. The thought of riding out into the ring in front of all those people was making my toes tingle. What if I made a mistake? What if Honey did one of her Waratah Grove performances and wound up bucking me off and sending me flying into the stands like a rag doll? What if I came last? At least my gear check and warm-up had gone well. I was hoping they wouldn't be the only things.

Finally it was my turn. Becky had gone long before me but I hadn't watched her ride. I'd never ridden in the same competition as her and I didn't want to freak myself out by watching the person I wanted to beat most in action.

Something had happened to me since Mrs Cho had taken our photo. It was a feeling that had started in my tummy as a prickle of annoyance and had grown into a big, fat, hairy ball of rage. I was angry. I was so angry with Becky. She hadn't even tried to see things from my point of view. What kind of best friend did that? I wanted to beat her. I wanted to beat her good and proper. Okay, so she was riding at Elementary level and I was a Preliminary. That wasn't the point. It was the score I was interested in and, as I gathered my reins, I sent up one of my prayers to the horse gods. Let my score be lower than Becky's. Please — I'll never ask you for anything ever, ever again if you let my score be lower.

I entered the ring as soon as the previous rider left. Honey was alert and calm. We completed a lap of the ring at a sitting trot, acknowledged the judge (who was sitting in the driver's seat of a parked car at C) then entered the arena at A.

I halted Honey at X and saluted the judge, taking both reins in my left hand, dropping my right hand to my side and bowing my head slightly. The judge waved at me from the car window.

I gave Honey the signal to proceed at a medium walk and she responded straight away. I had practised this walk with Honey over and over. It should be a free walk, I reminded myself, free and unconstrained. I walked her to C, concentrating hard on keeping her in a straight line, with her body parallel to the arena wall and listening for the sound of her hooves touching the ground in four equally spaced beats. I kept a light contact with her mouth, holding my hands steady.

We tracked right at C and I moved Honey into a working trot, knowing that, at Preliminary level, transitions were asked for between (not precisely at) markers and that I had a few strides to make sure Honey was doing what she was supposed to be doing. Honey's legs moved forward evenly past M and on to B. They were supposed to be moving forward 'elastically' as well, according to all the training I'd had at Waratah Grove. I smiled to myself, remembering Alex and Tash, surprised I hadn't had the words 'even and elastic' tattooed across my forehead (or anywhere else for that matter!).

We trotted on, past the F and on to A, then slowed back to a medium walk between A and K, then on to E where we turned right and halted at X. So far so good. Half the test was over and I was loving it. Dressage had always left me cold, but the Grove had changed all of that. Now I was hungry to advance. I couldn't wait to move up to Novice level and one day be competing as an Elementary. I couldn't wait to wear a top hat, but I knew that was years away.

I gave Honey the signal to walk again and we continued; left at B, medium walk to C, working trot between C and H; a left at H and then I halted Honey at G, faced the judge, held both reins in my left hand again, dropped my right hand and bowed my head. It was over and we had ridden like superstars. The crowd clapped for us and, as I looked up, I saw Pree standing on her seat doing what looked like a cross between 'I'm a little teapot' and laying an egg. She looked happy, though, which was a good sign. Then I noticed Becky sitting in the third row, watching me. Our eyes met but I looked away. When I was brave enough to look back, she was gone.

The novelty teams events were about to start. I was tired. No, I was exhausted! I felt like I'd been piggybacking Honey around dressage arenas and over showjumping courses. But I had to forget all about the pain in my back, my seat and my legs, because for most of the Riding Clubbers at the gymkhana, this was what it was all about. The individual events were a chance for everyone to prove how good a rider they were on their own merits. But it was only in the teams events that true supremacy could be decided. Pride was lost and won in the egg and spoon race, the potato race, the bottle race and the sack race. Every single member of Shady Creek Riding Club had come to the gymkhana with one purpose — to beat Pinebark Ridge in each event. Second place wouldn't do. We wanted the colour of our ribbons to match the colour of our shirts.

Bells started ringing and teams lined up. The Under 10s were first as usual and the Shady Creek riders screamed and cheered as our representatives crossed the finish line in first place, all eggs on spoons, three horse lengths ahead of Pinebark Ridge.

It was our turn next, the Under 12s. My team lined up, mounted, alongside Team Creep, Pinebark Ridge (Pree was riding for her club and waved madly at me) and Jacaranda Tops. Gary fussed like a mother chook, checking gear and spoons. While he was with the Creeps, I figured it might be a good time for a team pep talk. It was usually Becky's job, but she had been silent since the photo. She wasn't even speaking to the twins.

'We have one chance to kick butt in this race,' I began. Julie and Jodie were all ears. Becky stared off into the distance. 'We all love to smash Pinebark Ridge, but this race is about a lot more than that. It's about beating the Creeps.'

Jodie frowned and slapped Buttons's neck. 'What about Sandra? It's not her fault she got lumped with—'

'I know,' I said. Jodie was right, but it didn't matter how nice Sandra was. I couldn't bear to even think about the Creeps winning. 'But we have to do whatever we can. Becky? What do you reckon?'

Becky didn't flinch. She just kept staring.

'Becky?' I said again.

Julie held her reins in one hand and poked Becky's shoulder with the other. She turned around instantly, smiling. 'Yes, Julie?'

'Ash is talking to you,' Julie said, flicking a long strand of Boots's mane over his shoulder.

Becky looked confused. 'Is she? I didn't hear anything.'

'Becky, cut it out,' I said. 'We have to work together. This is a teams event, remember?'

Becky looked at the sky.

'What's wrong?' Julie asked.

'Nothing,' Becky said, sweetly. She leaned forward and stroked Charlie's neck as though everything were normal.

'Then stop ignoring Ashleigh — you guys are best friends.'

Becky shook her head. 'I don't have a best friend.'

Jodie's mouth fell open. Julie sucked in her breath.

'Becky, what's wrong with you?' I couldn't believe she was doing this to me. Not now.

Becky cupped her hand around her ear. 'Jodie, could you tell Ashleigh I can't hear a word she's saying.'

Jodie turned to me. 'Becky said to tell you—'

'I heard her loud and clear,' I snapped. 'Jodie can you tell Becky that I wouldn't want her for a best friend anyway. Best friends are there for each other no matter what. They don't dump someone for making one mistake.'

Jodie turned back to Becky. 'Becky, Ashleigh said—'

'Save it, Jodie.' Becky's smile was gone. I felt better knowing that I was upsetting her. I wanted her to know exactly how rotten I felt.

'Right. In order,' Gary shouted, reading from a list. 'Becky, you're number one, then Julie, Jodie and Ash. Don't forget that being Rider Four is a big responsibility, Ashleigh.'

That reminded me. I touched my helmet. Yep, my white band was on.

'Have you got your spoon?'

Becky held up our team's spoon.

'Have an egg.' Gary balanced a golf ball on the

spoon. 'Remember, don't touch it with anything but the spoon!'

Beside us Team Creep was getting into position — Flea in front, then Ryan and Sandra, and Carly was Rider Four. Carly met my eyes. She ran her index finger across her throat and laughed silently. I glared back at her. How I hated her sometimes.

The starter raised the bell. Becky watched him, ready to pounce on the course like a cat on a lizard. The spoon was secure in her left hand, her reins held tight in her right.

The bell rang and Becky burst out on Charlie. I sat quietly in the saddle. Usually I would have yelled and cheered for Becky. But there was nothing left inside me. She'd broken my heart and, while I wanted to win, I didn't care how well Becky rode any more. At least that's what I told myself.

Becky was back in no time and passed the spoon to Julie, who took it like she was picking up a tarantula, making sure her fingers were below the red tape. Boots took off leaving the Creeps to eat his dust.

'Go, Julie!' shrieked Jodie. She was trembling.

Julie and Boots bent left and right through the poles, but dropped the egg turning around the last pole.

'Pick it up!' Becky yelled.

Julie rode past the egg and leaned over in the saddle, poking at it with the spoon. She missed once, twice, then threw her right leg over the saddle, sliding to the ground. She scooped up the egg, scrambled onto Boots's back and was off again, but it was too late. Ryan, the Creep, was in front and so were Pinebark Ridge. The first rider from Jacaranda Tops was still walking the course, watching the egg like it was about to hatch.

'Julie, hurry!' Jodie screamed, watching over her shoulder as Ryan passed the spoon to Sandra. The Creeps lost a few seconds while Sandra paused to sneeze, but she cantered away from the starting line and through the course on Chocolate as though she was running the Golden Slipper.

Julie pulled up just as Sandra was bending around the second pole. Pree was out for Pinebark Ridge on her fat dun pony, Jasmine. Her team members were waving their hands, shouting and cheering. Jodie gripped her reins in one hand and held out the other one for the spoon. Julie held it out gingerly, conscious she was being watched by an official who was ready to attack at the first sign of even a fingernail above the red tape.

Jodie had a firm hold of the spoon. She drummed her heels on Buttons' sides and the gelding leapt into a canter.

'Go, Jodie!' I hollered, hoping I could push her along with voice power alone.

Jodie rode her best, bending close to the poles and tight around that last, treacherous turn, but it wasn't enough. Sandra was cantering back to Team Creep, holding out the spoon. Carly reached forward and took it perfectly, no fumble, not even a jiggle, and no fingers above the tape. Worse luck!

Pree handed over to Pinebark Ridge's Rider Four, who took off after Carly like his very life depended on it. Jacaranda Tops was out of the running — their Rider Two was still trying to pick up the egg from the saddle at the third pole.

I readied myself. Honey and I had competed all day. We were whacked but knew we had to give it our all just for a little longer. We might not be able to win, but we would go down fighting. I secured my reins in my left hand and raised it just a little way up Honey's neck. I sat deep in the saddle and gripped firmly with my thighs. I flexed the fingers of my right hand, waiting. Jodie was three horse lengths away, then two, one.

'Ash — take it!' Jodie shrieked. She held out the spoon handle. I took it carefully and, holding it away from me, I gave Honey the signal she'd been waiting for. Honey cantered towards the first pole. The egg jiggled but stayed snug in the spoon. On my right Carly thundered towards the finish line, a smile so huge on her face she made Luna Park look like a misery guts.

It didn't matter to me any more about beating the Creeps. Even if it had there was nothing I could do about it. The only thing I could still do was ride my best, not only for my team, but for Honey. She deserved that much.

We bent right around the first pole and approached the second pole. I shifted my seat and neck-reined to the left. Honey bent left around the pole. I shifted my weight again and she straightened up, cantering hard towards the third and final pole, the pole that had tripped up Julie. I slowed Honey right down, reining her in with one hand and held the egg out to one side. I reined Honey's nose tight around the pole and sighed with relief. We'd done it. A touch was all Honey needed. She cantered back through the poles and to the finish line. My heart sang with the joy of her speed and for those few seconds I had no worries in the world. I had nothing but love for my horse and the rhythm of her hooves beating along with my heart.

Team Creep (with poor Sandra's help) had won fair and square, followed by Pinebark Ridge and then us. Jacaranda Tops sent out their Rider Four just as I crossed the finish line.

'S'okay,' Jodie said, shrugging as I pulled Honey up to a halt and threw my egg and spoon into the open box near the starting line. 'Third's not bad. At least it's a ribbon.'

I leaned forward and clapped my hand on Honey's shoulder. She'd done well. I couldn't have asked for anything more. 'There's still the other races to go. I'm not all that bothered.'

'You should be,' Carly said, not even trying to contain her glee.

I rolled my eyes. 'Didn't your mother ever teach you it's rude to eavesdrop?'

'No,' Carly said.

Flea muscled forward on Scud. They are so made for each other. 'Where's your mummy, Spiller?'

My face burned. He sure knew which buttons to push. I'd tried my best all day to forget that Mum and Dad weren't here to watch me and just when I was feeling good he had to open his big mouth. 'Go tickle a redback.'

'Doesn't want to waste her time watching you lose? Or is she stuck at home with that brat?' Flea smirked, pleased with himself.

I felt sick. 'Leave my baby brother out of it.'

'Can't you pull the plug on that kid? It screams all night.'

'Missing out on beauty sleep are you, Fleabag?' I spat, rage coursing through my veins like electricity. 'You do need more than anyone else I know so I can see why you're upset.'

Flea booted Scud and the horse moved right beside Honey and me. Honey, in her obedience, didn't budge. I looked to my team. Nobody was putting on their superhero suits. I was going to have to fight this one alone.

'Talk to me like that again and I'll getcha!' Flea was furious. He made his hand into a fist and held it to my face.

I was frightened, but desperate not to show it. 'Get lost, will ya.'

Flea laughed. It seemed to be the signal Carly was waiting for and she moved Destiny close to my other side. Honey and I were firmly wedged between two Creeps. They were so close I couldn't move my legs. They were starting to hurt.

'Leave her alone,' Julie called at last.

Carly snorted. 'Who's gonna make us?'

'Ashleigh, what's happening?'

I struggled in my saddle and peered over Flea's shoulder. I could feel his stirrup iron digging into my ankle and Scud's side squashing my leg. Pree was mounted on Jasmine, watching with a stunned expression on her face.

I pushed Carly hard and she slipped in her saddle. Destiny swayed sideways, just enough for me to get Honey away. I trotted her to Pree, who held out her hand and grabbed Honey's bridle. It was then that the tears came.

'All of you can drop dead,' I said. I wiped at the tears that ran down my face. 'And you can stick Shady Creek Riding Club in your ears. I quit.'

Jodie's face fell. 'But the races? We still have three to go.'

I coughed, trying to push away the huge lump that was lodging in my throat. 'I don't care any more. I quit.'

I looked at Becky. She'd finally dropped her mask. She looked shocked. Good, I thought. I rummaged in the pocket of my jacket, pulled out a small box and threw it at Becky. 'Happy birthday.'

Her face went pale. She looked at the box, which had landed by Charlie's feet. Nobody did anything. Nobody said anything.

'C'mon, Ash,' Pree said softly. 'Let's get out of here.'

I nodded and left the starting line without looking back.

Pree stayed with me while I pulled myself together, then saw me safely out of the showground before returning to her team.

Lying in bed that night, the fallout from the day's events hit me with all the force of a fully loaded horse transporter. Without my best friend and Riding Club, I had nothing left in Shady Creek.

Twelve

Greener Pastures

It was getting colder. Winter was well and truly upon Shady Creek. The trees were bare and the sun didn't seem as bright.

It was Sunday, a Riding Club day, but I'd kicked my blue club shirt under my bed and wrapped myself up in my bright red Shady Trails Riding Ranch jacket instead. I slipped my left foot into my left stirrup and bounced into my saddle. Honey stood still and alert beneath me, her ears pricked forward.

'Good girl,' I murmured. 'You're a good girl, Honey.'

I gathered my reins and nudged Honey into a trot down the driveway.

When we'd first moved to Shady Creek I almost hyperventilated when I found out about Shady Creek Riding Club being on our street. Now I wished we'd never moved here. I loved our house and our land and Honey being with me every day, not like Princess, my riding school horse in the city whom I only saw once a week. But now that I was an ex-member of Riding Club I couldn't bear to ride past it. If flying had been an option I would have taken it. (No amount of wishing on stars or chicken wishbones had grown Honey a set of wings. Yet.) There was only one way to get to Shady Trails and that was straight down our street, past Riding Club and down the dirt road at the end of the block.

In the beginning, the day after the gymkhana, it had been easier. I was mad, and anger helps when you want to ignore your friends (and your enemies!). Now two weeks had passed and my anger had gone. All that was left was sadness for the way things used to be and the fear I could never have it back again. There was also pride. I had promised myself I would not be the one apologising to Becky, Julie, Jodie, Gary or anyone else. Yes, I'd let my team down when they needed me most, and I had suffered for it. But they'd let me face the Creeps on my own and I was having a lot of trouble forgiving them for that. I wasn't sure if I ever could.

I turned right at the end of the driveway. Honey moved instinctively into a canter. She knew how I felt. It was like there was a secret language that only the two of us understood. I could tell her everything with or without words. I could rest my forehead on hers and know that she understood everything.

The Shady Creek Riding Clubbers were all there, everyone but me. Pain twisted in my stomach. It hurt to see them there. It hurt not to be there. And most of all it hurt that Becky had dumped me for nothing. Riding Club had survived Shady Trails like I knew it would, brochures or no brochures. But the Horse Cents situation hadn't changed. Mum was still at home with Jason. Dad had still cut down his hours at the hospital to be with them, and Honey still needed to be fed, shod, wormed and immunised. And that was before tack, gymkhana and Riding Club fees, and everything I needed.

'Ash! Ash!'

I groaned. I couldn't believe my luck. I'd put my head down and scurried past before and hadn't been busted. I nudged Honey hard.

'Ash!'

I looked over my shoulder. Two familiar, identical faces were cantering after me. I rolled my eyes and gently pulled Honey to a halt.

Julie and Jodie bounced over on their ponies. Buttons dipped his head to graze the instant he was pulled up. Boots nipped Buttons on the neck. Julie slapped his shoulder.

'Behave, you!'

Boots stood still, Mr Meek and Mild, then dropped his head to the grass.

'Where are you going?' Jodie asked.

I shrugged. 'Work.' I looked down the road as though talking to Julie and Jodie was the last thing I wanted to do. We'd said nothing to each other at school since the gymkhana. They were a year below me but we'd sometimes hung around at lunchtime. The last two weeks had been lonely, but at least the Creeps had backed off. I'd heard from Pree that Gary had gone ballistic and assured Ryan, Flea and Carly that if any of them so much as blinked at me again they'd be banned from Riding Club for good.

'Aren't you coming to Riding Club?' Julie bit at her bottom lip, just the way I do when I'm nervous.

I shook my head. 'No.'

'But this will be the second meeting you've missed in a row. You never used to miss Riding Club.'

'I already told you guys. I quit.' I shifted in my saddle, uncomfortable, and was horrified to realise I'd never been uncomfortable in the saddle before.

Julie grimaced. 'You can't be serious about quitting.'

'I've never been more serious about anything in my life,' I said, pleased to see Jodie's face fall.

'What about us? The team? What are we supposed to do now?' Julie's ears were turning red. 'How can you just walk out and leave us one rider down? We can't compete in anything now.'

I bristled, shocked by her selfishness. 'Maybe someone should have thought about that before. Maybe someone should have helped me at the gymkhana.'

'We tried to help you!'

'When it was too late,' I snapped. 'Forget it. I'm never coming back. In fact . . .'

I had an awesome idea. I couldn't believe I hadn't thought of it before.

'I'm joining Pinebark Ridge.'

Julie's face drained of colour. 'You need your head read.'

I smiled, a tight cold smile. I knew I was being horrible but I didn't care. 'I don't actually. What I do need is to whip the saddles off Shady Creek Riding Club at the next gymkhana.'

Julie tugged at her sister's sleeve. 'C'mon, Jodes. We're wasting our time.'

Jodie wrenched Buttons's head up and the twins wheeled their ponies around, back in the direction of the club.

'If you ever come to your senses, you know where to find us,' Julie said over her shoulder. 'Good luck, Ashleigh.'

I watched them ride away and turned Honey back in the direction of Shady Trails before I could change my mind. Shady Creek Riding Club and me were history.

'Long time no Pree,' I announced, riding into the holding yard at Shady Trails. Pree looked up from the stirrup leather she was wrestling with and grinned. Her long black hair was weaved into its usual plait, the tail end curled like a piggy's.

'Ash! Help me with this leather, will ya?'

I kicked off my stirrups, threw my right leg over the saddle and slid to the ground, slipping Honey's reins over her ears. I handed the reins to Pree. 'Make room for the stirrup champion.'

Pree had been preparing Bartok for a pony lead. A tiny girl was balancing on the saddle and clinging to the pommel. I shortened the stirrups as much as I could but the leathers were still too long for her.

'Try this instead,' I said, pushing her boot into the leather itself. 'Rest your feet on top of the stirrups, okay?'

She nodded and giggled.

I wished Pree a nice pony lead and led Honey into the stable. She loved it at Shady Trails. A nice ride over, a quick groom, then off to the day paddock to make new friends, eat, roll and generally be a horse. She was untacked and in her headstall and I was checking her feet for stones when somebody cleared their throat.

'Mrs McMurray!' I lowered Honey's foot and placed it back on the ground gently.

Mrs McMurray was leaning on Honey's stall. She held her hand out to Honey. Honey touched her soft nose to Mrs McMurray's fingers and, sensing nothing in the way of treats, poked her nose into the trough instead.

'She's gorgeous, Ash. Your mum and dad must be so proud of the way you look after her, lovey.'

I shrugged. 'I guess so. They don't say much about it — they're so busy with the baby.' I clipped a lead rope onto Honey's headstall. She rubbed her face against my shoulder.

'I'd like to show you something,' Mrs McMurray said. 'In my office. Then you can see Sam for your schedule. Turn your girl out first, okay?'

'Okay.' I led Honey out of the stable, through the holding yard and out the back gate into the day paddock. Once we were deep enough inside the paddock, I unclipped her lead rope and slapped her rump. She set off at a trot and after choosing the leafiest, stickiest patch of dirt in Shady Trails, dropped to her knees and rolled, grunting with the pleasure of it.

I loped up to Mrs McMurray's office, curious. What could she have wanted to show me?

I knocked on Mrs McMurray's door and she called me in. She was sitting at her desk. The computer was on and she was surrounded by papers.

'Take a seat.' Mrs McMurray picked up one of the papers and held it out to me. 'I'd like you to have a think about this.'

'What is it?' I took the paper.

Mrs McMurray smiled. 'Only one way to find out.'

I looked at the paper. It was a glossy, folded brochure with a crest and lots of photos of smart-looking girls riding well-groomed horses.

'Linley Heights High School?' I raised my eyebrows.

'Have you heard of it?'

I nodded. 'Sure have. What horse mad girl hasn't heard of it?' Linley Heights was famous all over the country for being the only school where a girl could graduate with not only qualifications in Horsemanship but came out with a good chance of riding for Australia as well. One of the girls from South Beach Stables, my old riding school in the city, had started at Linley a few years ago. But her parents were rich.

'What do you think of Linley?' Mrs McMurray leaned forward, smiling at me.

I sighed. 'Sounds like a dream. Horsemanship, Equine Studies, riding every day. Who wouldn't think it's awesome?'

'Have you ever thought about enrolling?'

I shook my head. 'Mum and Dad can't afford it. I mean, I'd love to go. But I wouldn't even ask them. I'm going to Shady Creek and Districts High School next year. Like everybody else.'

Mrs McMurray smiled again. I had the feeling she knew something I didn't. 'There are scholarships, you know.'

Something started to tingle at the back of my neck. Scholarships? So there was one thing I'd never heard about Linley.

'Why don't you take that home and have a read? Maybe show your parents?'

I folded the brochure and slipped it into the pocket of my jacket. 'Why me?'

Mrs McMurray leaned back in her chair. 'It's one thing to love horses, Ash, love, and another still to ride well. But to live horses makes all the difference.'

I bit my lip, trying not to cry. She was right. I love horses and I ride okay. But the only thing I've ever wanted is to make horses my whole life. And there aren't too many people who understand that.

Thirteen

A Friend in Need

'So how was your last day?' Mum looked up from her baby bottle steamer. I slammed the back door behind me and threw my school bag into the corner of the kitchen.

'Not too bad. I'm totally glad it's holidays, but.' I opened the fridge listening hard for the sound of something irresistible calling my name. Unfortunately the fridge and its contents were silent.

Mum aimed a gentle kick at my backside. 'Close the fridge. All the cold air is freezing my feet.'

I let the door swing shut and wrenched open the pantry instead. 'Why is there never anything to eat in this house?'

'Did you give out your sleepover invitations? I left them on your desk this morning.'

Why is it that grown-ups never answer the important questions?

I shook my head. 'To who, Mum? Nobody's talking to me, remember? Besides, this way I get to eat all the pizzas myself.'

'Not on your life, Ash.' Mum sighed and filled the kettle with water. 'I don't know, possum. Can't you just say you're sorry and be done with it?'

'I'm not sorry.' I pulled out a loaf of bread and tossed it onto the bench. 'Where's the peanut butter?'

'Where it usually is.' Mum rummaged in the fridge for a moment while I selected a knife from the drawer. Mum handed me the peanut butter. 'I just think your life'll be easier if you get on Honey, ride over to Becky's and apologise. Then you can go back to Riding Club and have all your nice friends back. You're gonna live here a long time, Ash.'

I unscrewed the lid and took a deep breath. Hmmm. Peanut butter. I smeared enough onto a piece of bread to stick tiles to a wall and took a huge bite.

'Are you listening?' Mum tapped me on the head.

'Yizzarganoffy.'

Mum frowned. 'Subtitles, please.'

I swallowed hard and sucked a stray piece of peanutty bread from the roof of my mouth. 'I said, "Yes, but I'm still not sorry." I haven't done anything wrong, Mum. And besides, haven't you and Dad always taught me to stand up for what I believe in and always tell the truth?'

'Well, yes—' Mum began.

'Good,' I said, opening up the fridge again. I needed milk. Fast. 'Coz I'm not saying sorry, I don't care what happens. I'm not going back to Riding Club anyway. Pree's gonna introduce me at Pinebark Ridge next meeting.'

Mum shook her head. The kettle boiled and switched itself off. I finished my snack while she lined up six empty bottles on the bench and poured the same amount of boiling water into each one.

I drank my milk in two gulps and wiped my mouth with the back of my hand.

'That's disgusting,' Mum said, her eyebrows knitted together so hard they looked like arrows.

'How come whenever Jason does something disgusting it's cute?'

'Easy,' Mum said. 'He's nine weeks old. Everything he does is cute. When he's eleven going on twelve, I'm sure his cute status will be up for review.'

I dropped my knife and glass into the sink and wiped up the crumbs from the bench with a sponge while Mum measured sticky white powder from a huge tin into the bottles.

'Mum?'

'Yep?' Mum said, carefully scraping a knife along the top of the measuring scoop.

'I'm glad you're not so tired any more.'

Mum laughed. 'Not as glad as I am, kid.'

I picked up my bag from the floor and took a step towards the staircase. My hand wasn't even on the banister when the doorbell rang.

'Pumpernickel!' Mum said. 'Pumpernickel' is one of her favourite G-rated curses. 'Get that before they ring again, will you, Ash?'

I dropped my bag at the foot of the stairs and jogged down the hall to the front door. I wrenched it open. My heart stopped. Or at least it felt like it stopped. I couldn't breathe. I couldn't speak. All I could do was stand there with my hand on the doorknob and stare.

Becky was standing on the porch, tears running down her face. Her eyes were red and she was shaking. She opened her mouth. I thought she was going to say something, but she hiccupped and burst into a fresh wave of sobs.

'Becky!' I was stunned. 'What are you doing here? What's happened?'

Becky took a step towards me, shaking her head. She drew in a great rasping breath.

'Are you hurt?' I looked over my shoulder down the hall and into the kitchen. 'Mum!' She didn't answer.

Becky swallowed and closed her eyes. She seemed to be ordering herself to calm down.

'Becky, for goodness sake, tell me what's wrong!' I felt desperate.

Becky wiped her nose with the back of her hand. 'It's ... it's Cassata.'

My heart thumped. Had she been hurt? Was she sick? I wanted to know but didn't want to know all at once. 'What about her?'

'She's ... she's ...' Becky coughed and the tears fell again. 'She's been sold!'

'What?' I gasped.

'Oh, Ash!' Becky sobbed. She threw her arms around my neck and cried. I held her, crying with her. It couldn't be true.

'I can't believe it. I just can't believe it,' Becky sobbed.

'What happened?'

Becky and I sat on my bed, legs crossed, facing each other. We hadn't been together for such a long time. It was almost like a dream. Becky was here and we were talking to each other instead of fighting. But Cassata was gone.

Becky picked at my unicorn doona cover and sighed.

'Rachael's been complaining for ages that she doesn't have her own car.'

'Of course she doesn't. She's only fifteen.'

'She'll be sixteen in August. And when you're sixteen you can get your learner's, remember?'

I shrugged. I had no idea. I wasn't interested in cars. 'Go on.'

'She kept going on and on at Mum and Dad to buy her one but they said no. They said they never had cars bought for them when they were her age and if she wanted a car she had to raise the money herself.' Becky rubbed her eyes. Her hair fell forward hiding her face.

'Why didn't she just get a job?'

Becky looked up at the ceiling and inhaled hard through her nose. 'She has one. You know she works at the restaurant with me. She's just impatient. And selfish. She wanted all the money straight away.'

'When did it happen?' I patted Becky's knee. She burst into tears again.

'To-today. She was gone by the time I got home from school. Rachael knew I'd never let her go so she sold her behind my back. Now I'll never know who has her. I won't know if they're good or bad or if they even know anything about horses. I hate Rachael! I hate her!'

I lay back into my pillow. It was too much to take in. Cassata had been ripped from our lives, just like that. 'Who bought her?'

Becky wiped her face with her hands. 'Rachael says she doesn't know. She said it was some guy with a float that already had a horse inside. She doesn't care, anyway. All she was interested in was getting her money. Now she can buy her stinky old car and I hope she rots in it.'

'What did your mum and dad say?'

'Dad's so angry. He's been in the garage all afternoon. Mum was crying. I mean, she doesn't ride or anything, but Cassata and Mum were mates.'

Becky flopped down beside me. We lay side by side, silent, for a while. That's the way it is with best friends. Sometimes when you say nothing, you're saying the most important things of all.

I closed my eyes and rested my head against Becky's. I was so relieved to have her back.

'Ash?' Becky said eventually.

'Hmm?' I didn't want to speak. I was too tired. The news about Cassata had drained me. It was like someone had drilled a hole in my heart and all my energy, all my fight, had leaked out.

'Ash, I'm so sorry.'

I sat upright and looked down at Becky, not sure what to say. Becky tugged at her eyebrow and licked her lips before sitting up to face me.

'I ... I ... I shouldn't have done what I did to you. I dunno, I just lost it. After a while it was all too big, like I'd climbed up a cliff and didn't know how to get back down.'

'I'm sorry, too,' I said, grabbing her hand. 'I said some pretty mean things to you. And I should never have gone behind your back with those brochures. Best friends should trust each other.'

Becky squeezed my hand. 'I never want to fight with you again. It's been so totally horrible these last few weeks.'

I smiled. 'Tell me about it.'

Becky put her hand to her throat. 'And thank you.'

I frowned. 'For what?'

Becky tugged at something silver. 'For my present. It's so beautiful. I haven't taken it off.'

She was wearing the silver chain with the horse I'd bought her for her birthday. Tears burned my eyes again. I hugged her, hard, never wanting to let go. Becky hugged me back. It was aweome.

I heard Jason squeak, then cry and Becky let me go.

'Is that the baby?'

I winked. 'Nah.'

Becky pushed me. Her face was pale and stained with tears, but I distinctly saw the hint of a smile. 'Nong! Can I see him? It's been ages.'

I nodded. 'Course you can.'

I slid off the bed and grabbed her hand, dragging her out of my room, down the hall and into Jason's room. The curtains were open and he was lying in his cot in his baby suit. He looked like a blue banana. We peeked over the side of the cot. Jason looked up at us and smiled.

'Didja see that, Ash?' Becky said. 'He's smiling at us!'

'It's probably gas. Believe me, the kid has bowels like a moo cow.'

Becky offered Jason her finger, which he was ecstatic to hold and squeeze. He gave her another gummy smile.

'He likes me,' Becky murmured, gazing at him. 'Do you reckon I should ask Mum and Dad for a baby?'

'Are you sick? Look at the trouble Rachael's causing.'

'She's not a baby, Ash.'

'But she was one once.'

Becky shook her head. 'I just don't get it. How could she have done it? People don't sell their dogs or cats.'

'How about their baby brothers?'

'Ash, don't be a hoof-head.'

Becky prised Jason's fingers from hers. He jerked his arms around, a bit like he was pretending to be a pair of windscreen wipers. I let the side down on the cot, bent down and scooped him up. He burped, then sighed and rested his chin on my shoulder.

'Becky, everything's gonna be all right.'

Becky shook her head. 'How can you say that? Nothing'll ever be all right, ever ever.'

I swayed from side to side patting Jason's back, just like Mum does.

'We're gonna get her back, Beck,' I said. I looked into her eyes. 'We're gonna find her and bring her home. I promise you.'

Becky sniffled, then nodded. A single tear trickled down her cheek. 'Okay.'

I sighed. 'Okay.'

Jason burped again. It was unanimous.

Fourteen

Horse Heist!

'Rachael may be an idiot but at least she had the sense to sell Cassata at the end of the term. If we were at school, we'd never find her.' Becky fidgeted with her reins, running them through her fingers again and again. When she was done fidgeting she chewed hard on each of her fingernails.

I was glad Gary wasn't here to see her — he had enough to worry about without watching his own daughter throw everything he'd ever taught her about riding in the muck-out heap. I'd never seen Becky like this. She looked like she hadn't slept for days. Her face was pale and there were dark circles under her eyes.

'Good to see you're looking on the bright side,' I said, grimacing. As far as I was concerned there was no bright side. Cassata was gone, Rachael was already searching the Net for a car and Becky and I still had no idea how to get our sweet Appaloosa back. Okay, so she was really the Chos' horse, but she was mine too, in a way. I'd ridden Cassata until Becky and I had found Honey and rescued her. And she'd spent the summer at my place. It's also a truth universally acknowledged that any horse of my best friend is also a horse of mine.

I leaned forward and patted Honey's neck. Honey snorted and chomped on her bit. I could tell she was itching for a run. 'Chill out, Honey horse. We're thinking.'

It had been too long since Becky and I had been on a trail ride together. It wasn't a new trail, but it was one of our favourites. Anyway, the whole trail ride gig had been a huge diversion. What we really had planned for the day wasn't to lope around Shady Creek together, but to formulate a foolproof horse retrieval plan and we needed to throw our parents off the scent. Especially mine. They seemed to have developed Ashleigh's-about-to-get-herself-in-trouble detectors and I was certain once they got even the faintest whiff of a scheme they'd nip it in the bud faster than you can say 'busted'. Besides, with Rachael's moods (unparalleled guilt, according to Becky, which often led directly to missiles being launched at younger sisters and their best friends), Becky's house was fraught with danger and chock-a-block full of grown-up ears and big sister mouth.

'Has Rachael been able to remember anything else about the guy?'

Becky shook her head, gnawing on her thumbnail. It's a good thing Charlie is such a legend. He ambled down the trail calm as a rocking horse, despite his mistress's super stress.

'She gave me this.' Becky pulled a white card out of her jacket pocket and handed it to me. 'She found it on the lawn.'

I looked at the card. It was a bit crumpled and was stained with what looked to be tomato sauce. '*Paul Burton. Horse Dealer.*'

'There's a phone number. All we have to do is call this Paul Burton guy, tell him we want Cassata and pay him what he paid Rachael,' Becky said.

She smiled at me, her eyes bright for the first time in days. It all seemed so easy.

'What did he pay Rachael?' I was almost too frightened to ask. I had a few hundred dollars in Horse Cents and I'd hand it all over to get Cassata back in less than a heartbeat. But what if I couldn't afford her? I wasn't going to ask Mum and Dad for money. They were always complaining about how much nappies cost and about banks breathing down their necks. And from what Becky had told me, with the restaurant and everything else, the Chos couldn't buy Cassata back either.

'He gave her a cheque for three thousand dollars,' Becky said.

'What?' I gasped. I couldn't believe it.

Becky nodded. 'I was totally freaked when Rachael told me. I mean, Cassata's worth heaps more than that, but the guy said he wouldn't pay because Cassata's so unfit. All dealers want to make a profit in the end, anyway.'

I was freaked as well. There was no way I'd ever be able to raise three thousand dollars. Not in my lifetime, anyway. I tangled my fingers in Honey's mane and shivered knowing that the only way we'd ever be able to get Cassata back was by either convincing Rachael to tear up the cheque or hoping that Paul Burton had forgotten how much he'd paid for her.

We let ourselves in to the Shady Creek Riding Club office using the spare key Gary always kept jammed into the toe of a shaggy old boot he'd nailed to the wall to use as a letterbox. Becky (and now me) was the only one who knew where it was. Gary's great at finding hiding places for all sorts of things but not so great at remembering where they are.

The office was in its usual state of 'just-hit-by-a-cyclone', Gary-style organisation. There were papers piled high on the desk, old horseshoes scattered across the floor, rusty old bits spilling out of an even rustier baby formula tin and an old saddle resting against the wall that looked like it had had a role to play in the Eureka Stockade.

I hadn't ever spent much time in Gary's office (apart from a brief moneymaking spell just after we'd moved to Shady Creek) but Becky was quite comfortable.

'The phone's in here somewhere,' she said, scanning the room.

'I didn't even know there was a phone,' I said.

Becky put her hands on her hips. 'You've just gotta know where to look.'

We searched under papers and behind the saddle.

'Maybe if we wait for it to ring—'

'We need it now.' Becky was beginning to panic.

I tripped over something. It was a cord! I picked up the cord and followed it to a bucket under the desk. The phone was wrapped up in a pair of old joddies.

Becky called the number on the card and spoke with Paul Burton. By the look on her face, it wasn't good news.

Becky hung up the phone. 'This can't be happening,' Becky said, her elbows on the desk and her hands over her face. 'It's like some nightmare.'

'What's going on?' I said, shaking my head.

'He's never been to Shady Creek. He said he's never heard of Rachael Cho and doesn't know anything about an Appaloosa mare.'

In the space of one phone call we'd fallen into more trouble than we could have imagined.

We were stunned. There was no way we could ever have seen this coming. If Paul Burton had never been to Shady Creek, who had taken Cassata? And how did his card wind up on the Chos' front lawn?

Becky slumped in Gary's chair, the phone resting in her lap. Then she slapped her hand to her mouth and sat bolt upright. Her eyes were wide.

'What? What is it?' I looked behind me expecting to see one of the Creepketeers darkening the doorstep, or worse, all of them. There was no one there.

Becky shoved the phone back into the bucket. 'We've gotta get home. Now!'

'Why?' I was starting to get scared.

'No t-time to tell you,' Becky stammered. 'Gotta go home.'

She rushed past me and leapt into the saddle, looking over her shoulder to see where I was.

'Ashleigh, what are you doing?'

I shook my head and slammed the office door shut, wedged the key back into the toe of the boot and scrambled into the saddle. I'd had barely enough time to settle my bottom down when Charlie sprang into a canter across the Riding Club paddock and out of the gate. Honey and I followed at a messy canter with me clinging to the pommel and trying to shove

179

my feet into the stirrups at the same time. We rode on and on, over lawns and across driveways, until at last we pulled up outside Becky's house. Becky threw me Charlie's reins and ran down the front path to her door. She disappeared inside. I led the horses to the corral, quickly untacking them and rubbing them down with an old scrap of towel. I checked that the water trough was full and bolted for the house.

Becky, Rachael and Mrs Cho were sitting around the kitchen table. Becky was crying. Rachael's face was buried in her hands. Mrs Cho looked up when I knocked on the back door. Her eyes were wet.

'Hi, Ash sweetie,' she said, trying to smile. I could tell she was pretending not to be upset. 'It's been a long time!'

'It has,' I said. I was terrified. The room was quiet apart from the sound of Becky sobbing. I didn't know where to look or what to do. Suddenly I wanted to go home.

'We've had some news,' Mrs Cho said. 'About Cassata.'

My stomach clenched. I sat at the table with them and shoved my fingers into my mouth, biting at my nails.

'We had a call from the police earlier,' Mrs Cho said. 'Apparently there's a thief operating in the area, offering to buy horses and handing over cheques—'

'That bounce!' Rachael wailed.

'Just shut up, Rachael!' Becky shrieked. I jumped in my seat. 'You're more upset about not getting your lousy three grand than you are about losing Cassata.'

'Girls!' Mrs Cho said. Her cheeks reddened. 'Haven't we all had enough for one day?'

'But it's true, Mum,' Becky cried. 'She doesn't care about anything but getting her stupid car.'

Rachael pushed back her chair with a screech and ran from the room. Her footsteps pounded down the hallway and then a door slammed.

'Becky,' said Mrs Cho. 'I expect you to calm down and apologise to your sister. She's had to learn a very difficult lesson.'

'But what about Cassata?' I said. 'Where is she?'

Becky wiped her face with the back of her hand. 'The police said she's been stolen. And not just her, heaps of horses from around here. This guy goes around gathering them up and dumps them at the nearest saleyard. By the time the owners figure out they'll never see their money, he's long gone and so are their horses.'

'It can't be true,' I said. I felt weak, flat. I couldn't believe there were actually people in the world like that. People who didn't care how much they hurt others or what they took as long as they got what they wanted. It had never occurred to me that a horse could be stolen, ever. Especially a horse I knew, in my home town. I wondered for a moment what Mum and Dad would say to keeping Honey inside the house at night.

Mrs Cho sighed, shaking her head. 'There's nothing we can do now. Cassata could be anywhere, with anyone. Let's just hope she hasn't fallen into the wrong hands.' Mrs Cho got up and opened the pantry. 'Are you girls hungry? Becky, you haven't eaten all day.'

Becky rolled her eyes. 'How can you talk about food at a time like this?'

'What sort of wrong hands?' I said. 'What do you mean?'

Mrs Cho pulled a loaf of bread from the pantry and set it down on the bench. She opened up her cupboard and slid out the breadboard then set about making sandwiches for Becky and me.

'Please, Mrs Cho.' I could tell she was trying to hide something from us.

'Ashleigh,' she said, spreading butter on what seemed like enough slices of bread to feed an army, 'just forget what I said. I'm sure Cassata will have found a loving home with some sweet girl, just like you two.'

'But—' I began.

'She means the doggers!' I twisted around. Rachael was standing in the doorway, her face streaked with tears.

Mrs Cho slammed down her knife. 'Rachael, please!'

'They have to know the truth, Mum. They're not babies.'

Becky stood up. 'What's a dogger?'

My heart began to pound. Whatever it was, it didn't sound like a sweet little girl.

'Rachael!' Mrs Cho warned. Her lips were so thin I could barely make them out. Rachael crossed her arms and flicked her hair over her shoulder with a toss of her head.

The back door opened and Gary walked into the kitchen.

'What's going on?' he said. 'Oh, hi, Ash!'

'Dad, what's a dogger?' Becky said at once.

'It's a knackery owner. Why?'

'Oh, Gary!' Mrs Cho said. She threw her arms up.

'What? What have I done now?' Gary picked up a slice of buttered bread and took a bite.

'Dad, we have to find Cassata,' Becky said, shrilly.

Gary shook his head. 'The police seem to think it's impossible.'

'It's not!' Becky's eyes were wide. I knew she was about to start crying again. 'Dad, c'mon. You know heaps of people who could help us.'

'What d'you think I've been doing all day?' Gary was angry. I'd seen him mad at the Creeps, but never at Becky. 'I've called everyone, everywhere. No one's seen an Appaloosa mare. I've done all I can, Becky.'

'There has to be something we can do,' she cried. 'We can't just let her disappear.'

Gary's face softened and he pulled Becky into his arms. 'There's nothing more I can do, Beck. I've given it as much time as I can. I have a business to run.'

Becky pulled away from her father and looked into his face, saying nothing. She shook her head slowly, turned and ran from the kitchen. I followed her to the sound of Mrs Cho telling Rachael how irresponsible she had been lately.

I found Becky outside sitting on the corral fence watching Honey and Charlie nibbling at a haynet. The wind was blowing her hair. She looked really pretty.

'Becky?' I said. 'Are you okay?'

Becky shrugged. 'I don't know.'

'We'll get her back, Beck. I promised you we would, and I meant it.' I climbed onto the fence and sat beside her. She leaned into me and I wrapped my arm around her. Her body shook as she cried.

'A knackery! What if she wound up at a knackery? Oh, Ash, what am I gonna do?'

As we sat together Becky cried herself out. Something began ticking over in my brain. An idea. An incredibly brilliant idea. Operation Cassata was about to be unveiled.

Fifteen

Operation Cassata

'That you, Ash?'

'Who else? You ready?'

Becky, wrapped in a thick winter jacket, rode out from underneath a tree on her front lawn, yawning as wide as a hippo. Honey stretched out her neck to Charlie and the horses touched nostrils in greeting.

'C'mon,' I whispered, shivering. I hadn't realised it would be so cold. 'We've gotta get going before they miss us. Did you write your note?'

Becky nodded stiffly. '"Dear Mum and Dad, me and Ash have gone for an early morning hack, back for lunch, love Becky." Just like you said. I still can't believe I agreed to this.'

I pressed my finger to my lips. 'Have you swallowed a subwoofer?'

The last thing I wanted was to wake up the Chos. They'd been through enough over the last few days without finding Becky missing from her bed at four in the morning. But it was our one chance, our only chance, to get to the saleyards in Maclay before the day's auctions began. It was the biggest and busiest in the whole region. If we were going to find Cassata, I was sure we'd find her there. The Maclay Livestock Sales website had said all auctions were held on the first Tuesday of every month at eight sharp. Maclay was at least a three-hour ride away. As long as we didn't get busted first.

'Sorry!' Becky whispered. 'I didn't get much sleep last night, uh, this morning. You know what I mean. I was just too stressed.'

I tugged gently on Honey's left rein and nudged her sides slightly. She took her first step on our long journey and Charlie followed suit.

We rode at a walk down the empty streets in silence, every now and then passing through the small orange pools given off by the streetlights. How do you train a horse to tiptoe? I wondered.

It wasn't long before we were clear of Shady Creek and were riding down the highway that tipped the very edge of town and linked it to all the other towns up and down the coast. I'd never ridden Honey here before.

'You scared?' Becky asked.

I nodded. 'Of course I am.'

'I was hoping you wouldn't say that.'

The sky was blue-black and bursting with stars. I knew then why I'd never seen too many stars in the city — they'd been here in Shady Creek the whole time. The moon was high and so round and bright. I could see everything. It all looked magical and silvery. Honey's white blaze shone in the moonlight. Her coat gleamed, bouncing moonbeams back to the clouds. I felt that we four were the only beings on Earth.

'Sure it's this way?' I muttered to Becky.

She nodded, stiffly. 'Course I'm sure. I've only been to Maclay a hundred thousand times. If only Dad didn't have rocks in his head, he could be driving us there instead of making us drag these guys all the way.'

'I still can't believe he said no. How many times did you ask him?'

'Well ...' Becky said. She rubbed her hands together and blew into them.

'Becky?'

My best friend mumbled something under her breath. I strained my ears.

'What was that?'

'I said, I never asked him.'

I felt like I'd been smacked in the guts with a bag of pony pellets. 'Becky!'

'He would have said no, anyway. You heard him — he's got a business to run.' Becky pulled a horrible face, impersonating Gary.

'But, he might—'

'No!' Becky's eyes were wild. 'You don't know him like I do. He makes mules look cooperative. Listen, didja bring the—'

'Money.' I patted my zipped-up jacket pocket. 'It's all here.'

Although Cassata wasn't mine, I loved her so much. If it took every single cent of my Horse Cents fund I was happy to pay it to get her back.

'Hungry?' I asked, thinking of the goodies I'd packed into my saddlebag.

Becky shook her head. 'Nuh. I just wanna get there.'

I looked over my shoulder, watching for a moment as the *Welcome to Shady Creek* sign grew smaller and smaller. 'Well, let's go, then.'

Becky raised her hand. I did likewise and we high-fived, then gathered our reins and, now that the horses were warmed up and ready, urged them into a canter. Cassata could be waiting for us to rescue her and there wasn't a moment to lose.

'If my backside wasn't so numb it'd be killing me.' I wriggled in my saddle, trying to relocate my weight to a patch of backside that wasn't aching. I didn't usually get saddle sore, but the cold early morning air had made every part of my body stiff.

'Your backside'll live,' Becky said, rolling her eyes. 'I hope we can say the same for those poor horses!'

We had pulled up our horses in front of the Maclay Livestock Sales gates. It was busy. There were dozens and dozens of horses and ponies of all shapes and sizes penned in holding yards. Grown-ups, mostly men wearing hats, stalked from yard to yard with clipboards and pens. Every now and then one of them poked a horse or pulled at its ear. At least, as Becky said, they were interested (sort of) in the health of the horses. Maybe they intended their purchases for riding schools or reselling.

We spotted the doggers straight away. They were the ones who didn't touch the horses and barely even looked at them. They just scribbled on their papers, nodding slightly to the people around them. A few handed cash over to a man in a blue long-sleeved shirt and led horses to their trucks, one after another.

'I hate them,' Becky hissed. 'I hate them all. Who could do that to a horse?'

I shook my head feeling a bitter taste in my mouth. I couldn't answer Becky's question. I couldn't understand the doggers at all.

'I wish I was rich,' I said, rubbing my frozen fingers into Honey's neck, feeling her warmth, her vitality, and loving her so much my chest hurt. 'I wish I could win the lottery. Then I'd come back here and buy them all. I'd save every one of them, Beck.'

'Can you see her?'

We stood up in our stirrups, groaning, and scanned the yards. There were bays, duns, blacks, greys, chestnuts, even a palomino. But there was no sign of an Appaloosa.

'Maybe she never wound up here.'

'Not likely,' Becky said. 'The guy would have dumped her here. Why drag a horse all over the country? Better to sell her quick smart, take the money and run.'

'So where is she?' I said. 'We're right on time. The auctions haven't even started yet.'

Becky covered her face with her hands. 'Let me think! We need to rest and water these two. And we need to get closer. She could be tucked away in there somewhere. Or she could be in a truck.'

I shook my feet from my stirrups, threw my right leg over the left side of my saddle and slid to the ground. Prickly pins and needles charged up and down my legs. I shook them urgently, trying to make it stop. 'What are we waiting for?'

Ten minutes later Honey and Charlie were tied to a tree drinking deeply from a begged bucket, their saddles thrown over branches, their damp saddlecloths flapping in the breeze. We'd rubbed them down with handfuls of straw from the ground, cursing ourselves for not having brought towels.

'D'you think they'll be all right here?' I said, looking over my shoulder at Honey and Charlie. 'What if someone thinks they're for sale?'

'They'll have me to deal with,' Becky muttered, hooking her arm through mine and steering me headfirst into a sea of people.

We ducked through the crowd, picking up snippets of conversations about droughts and hand-feeding and the government. My heart was thumping. We were the only kids here. I was sure it wouldn't take long for someone to pick us up by the seats of our joddies and turf us out over the gates. As long as we had time to find Cassata and buy her back, that was all that mattered.

Within half an hour we'd covered the place scanning every yard and truck. Cassata was nowhere to be found.

'Him,' Becky said, pointing at the man in blue we'd seen accepting money earlier. He was leaning against a holding yard, arms folded across his chest. The yard was packed with ponies. Some were thin and miserable looking. Others had shiny coats and bright eyes. One even had a plaited tail. I couldn't help but wonder if they'd been stolen as well. 'We have to ask him. I bet he's seen her.'

The auction had started and a man's voice babbled in the loudspeakers. '*Do I hear a hundred? Do I hear one fifty?*' We weaved our way through the crowd and stood in front of him, looking up into his face. He was tall and wide and his face was wide as well. His skin was tanned and his nose was red. He seemed to be some sort of official. *Maclay Livestock Sales* was embroidered onto the chest pocket of his shirt.

Becky cleared her throat.

'Excuse me?'

The man didn't look down. Either he was very hard of hearing or completely ignoring us. We get a bit used to that, us kids, but we had no time to be ignored.

Becky tugged on his shirtsleeve. 'Excuse me?'

The man looked down and arched one thick eyebrow. I didn't know whether to be impressed or terrified. I turned and leaned against the wall of the holding yard, my hands wringing behind my back. Something warm and wet was thrust into my hands. I jumped and turned around. Looking up at me was a gorgeous dark brown miniature pony with a black mane and tail. He pushed his head through the bars and nickered. I held my hands up, open. I had nothing to give him. It was a terrible feeling. I knew what fate could be awaiting him and I couldn't even offer him a slice of carrot. All I could do was rub behind his ears. His eyes closed and he leaned hard against the fence.

'What is it?' the man said.

Becky squeezed my arm. 'We're looking for Cassata.'

The man laughed. 'You're in the wrong place, kid. Isn't that some kind of dessert?'

Becky shook her head. 'She's a horse, an Appaloosa mare. She was picked up a few days ago in Shady Creek. We think she might have been brought here.'

The man tipped his hat back and rubbed at his hairline. 'Appaloosa mare? We've had a ton of horses through here in the last few days. Hmmm. Ah yes! I remember that mare. She's gone.'

Becky's face drained of colour. I thought she was going to faint.

'You can't be serious,' she said. 'Gone where?'

'Sold her to a dealer. Comes by once a month to pick up horses. Fixes 'em up and sells 'em on. That's what happens here, kid.'

Becky grabbed onto the fence, shaking her head. I wrapped my arm around her shoulders.

'A dealer's better than a dogger, Beck,' I whispered.

She nodded slightly. I had to get her out of there.

'Thank you,' I said to the man. I began to steer Becky away.

'Wait,' he called.

I turned back. He was digging in his pocket. 'The guy's pretty reputable. Here's his card. Reckon you'd be finding your mare if you get onto him fast enough.'

I accepted the card and pushed it into the pocket of my jacket. Becky coughed. She was crying again. The man turned his back to us and looked out over the yard of ponies. The mini was watching me. I imagined him herded into a slaughterhouse and felt sick with guilt.

'Mister,' I said. 'What's going to happen to this pony, the miniature?'

He shrugged. 'Same as the others. If I can't sell 'em on after a month they go to the warehouse.'

'How could you?' Becky sobbed.

'Business is business, girls.'

'How long's he been here?' I asked, my arm beginning to ache from the weight of supporting Becky.

''Bout three weeks, I'd reckon.' The man squinted up at the sky, thinking. 'Godwin was my last dealer this month.'

'And nobody wanted him?' I was amazed. He was so beautiful.

'Nuh. He's unbroken, bit of a wild one. Ponies like that are hard to sell on. People want rocking horses for their kids and he ain't no rocking horse.'

'But he's so sweet.'

The man turned to leave. 'Nice chatting with you girls, but I gotta get back to work.'

'How much is he?' I blurted out. Becky recovered instantly.

'Ash, what are you doing?' she hissed.

The man smiled. 'How much you offering?'

I thought for a second. 'Fifty.'

The man laughed and shoved his hands deep into his pockets.

'All right, seventy-five then.'

Becky tugged at my arm. 'Ash, stop it.'

I pulled my arm away. I knew what was bugging her. The Horse Cents money. I was supposed to be spending it on Cassata. I knew we had to save her. But it was my money. And I wanted to save the little pony as well.

'You're wasting my time.' The man turned again and took a step away.

'A hundred,' I called after him.

'Ashleigh! Cut it out!' Becky was frantic.

The man stopped again, and grinned at me. 'One twenty-five and he's yours.'

'One fifteen.'

He nodded. 'You're good at this, kid. One twenty and I'll throw in a headstall and lead rope. I reckon you'll need one.'

'Sold.' I held out my hand and he pumped it.

The man opened the gate and unhooked a tiny headstall and lead rope from the top rung of the fence. I dug in my pocket for the money. Becky whacked my arm. 'I can't believe you just did that.'

'Becky, they'll sell him to the doggers. You heard what the guy said.'

Becky folded her arms. 'He probably only said

198

that to make you buy him. We need that money for Cassata.'

'One twenty isn't going to make much difference.'

The gate opened again and the man emerged holding the mini tightly by the headstall. We made the swap, money for the pony, and he was mine. I kneeled down and hugged him tight. He nuzzled my neck, snorting. He was so cute. I hadn't been this happy since the day I'd found out Honey was going to be mine forever.

I stood up and prepared to lead him out of Maclay Livestock Sales, standing close to his near shoulder, which came up to my hip, with my right hand on the rope near his headstall and my left hand holding the slack. Before I'd taken even one step the mini jerked the rope from my right hand and ran in circles around me, tangling me good and proper.

'Great, Ash. How are we gonna get back home before dark with a mini?' Becky was scowling.

I gulped — I hadn't thought of that. 'But how could I leave him here? You know what would have happened to him.'

'What about what's happening to Cassata? Isn't that why we came all this way?'

'All we can do is try,' I said, stepping out of the loops of lead rope. 'I can always sit him up on Honey with me.'

Becky managed a smile. 'That I'd like to see. Now let's get out of here.'

We made our way back to our horses, who both stared at the curious pony I was dragging, and began our journey home. The mini danced in front of Honey, dashing this way and that, as far as the lead rope would allow. Honey shied as he tried to run under her belly.

'I can't do it,' I said at last, pulling Honey up and sliding down from the saddle. 'I'll have to lead them both home.'

Becky moaned. 'We're not even halfway. I told you this would happen, didn't I?'

Considering I was prepared to spend my entire Horse Cents fund to get Cassata back, Becky was being less than supportive of my decision to save the mini. 'You go. I'll walk them back.'

'I can't leave you here,' Becky said. 'It's way after lunch. We promised to be home by now.'

I shrugged. 'What do you want me to do? Just let

him go? You go home and ring Mum and Dad for me. Tell them I'll be late.'

Becky's face softened. 'I've got a better idea. Just trust me, okay?'

I watched her canter down the highway, and kept walking — Honey on my left side, the mini on my right.

'What am I going to call you?' I asked him. 'Mini? That's not such a great name, is it?' He trotted beside me, his mane bouncing with every step.

We walked on and on, stopping every now and then for a rest and a snack — grass for the horses, a biscuit or an apple for me. I shared the core between the two of them.

Nearly three hours after Becky had ridden away, a four-wheel drive towing a familiar-looking horse float pulled up beside me. Gary was behind the wheel. Dad was in the front passenger seat, a tight look on his face. Becky opened the back door and jumped down to the ground.

'Your dad's ropable, Ash. But in a relieved kind of way.'

'He can't be more relieved than me,' I said.

Becky took Honey's reins from my hand and led her into the float. Gary appeared at my side and scratched the mini on his head.

'What's his name?' Gary said.

I smiled, climbing into the back seat. 'Toffee.'

Gary closed the door and I lay down. Dad peered over the front seat.

'What have you got to say for yourself, Ashleigh Louise?'

'Hi, Dad,' I mumbled, sleep coming to claim me so fast I could barely hold it at bay.

'We'll talk about this when we get home, Miss.'

'No worries.'

Becky appeared on the seat beside me. The engine started and I closed my eyes. It wasn't long before I fell asleep, happy in the knowledge that I was on my way home and my horses were safe at last.

Sixteen

Hobby Horse

'What's with you, Ash? You've been off with the pixies all morning.'

'Huh?'

Pree frowned and laid the back of her hand across my forehead. 'Feels like you have a fever. Maybe it's malaria.'

I rolled my eyes and ran the body brush over Bartok's round rump. He needed a good groom, a feed and to be turned out. It's not easy being a Riding Ranch pony in the school holidays. 'I don't have malaria.'

What I did have was Cassata-rescue-plan anxiety. Now that our parents no longer trusted us outside a

5-metre radius of our homes, Gary and Dad were in on the plans. I had every right to be nervous — grown-ups always seem to mess things up.

'Are you sure? If you've got a fever it could be anything. I was reading one of Dad's journals last night and there was this really disgusting picture of a—'

'Pree, please!' I closed my eyes and covered my ears with my hands, so grossed out I was still holding onto the body brush. I can handle horses that foal, cuts on legs, mud fever, colic or even laminitis. But bring humans into the equation and I get a bit woozy.

'What?' Pree was wide-eyed. 'Don't forget my dad's a doctor.'

'Well my dad's a nurse,' I grumbled. 'Anyway, I'm not sick, it's this horse. Cassata.'

'Did you get her back?' Pree leaned on her shovel and watched me. I sighed and told her the whole story from start to finish.

'Wow.' Pree was impressed. 'I can't believe you do things like that. My mum and dad would have flipped their lids.'

'You think mine didn't? I'm grounded.'

'But you're here.' Pree raised her eyebrows quizzically.

'Work is one thing, play is another.'

'Like anyone'd call this work! Isn't this job a dream come true? I mean, I always wanted to work with horses but this is unbelievable. Hey, what has four frogs but doesn't croak?'

I shrugged. 'I give up.'

'A horse!' Pree cracked up laughing. 'D'you get it? A horse! It has frogs, in its feet! So, what's next? With Cassata, I mean.'

I checked for eavesdroppers, peeking over the stall walls. 'We've found the dealer. There's a horse auction tomorrow and we're going to buy Cassata back.'

'Just Cassata?' Pree smiled knowingly. 'Or are you planning to add another horse to the Ashleigh Miller collection?'

'Just Cassata.' I smiled. 'But Toff's so worth it. He'll be perfect for Jason—'

'Wait a minute,' Pree said suddenly. 'If you're grounded how are you getting to the auction?'

'Becky's dad's taking us and my dad's coming too.'

Pree picked up her shovel and scooped up a nice round pile of manure. 'Don't forget I have to take

205

you over to Pinebark Ridge Riding Club. You know, show you round.'

I was afraid she'd bring that up. It was true, I'd promised her I'd join Pinebark Ridge and at the time I'd really truly meant it. But now Becky and I had made up I didn't really want to join Pinebark Ridge any more. But I didn't want to let Pree down either. She'd been nothing but nice to me since the first day we'd met. And she'd been the only person from either club to come to my rescue at that terrible gymkhana. I didn't know what to do.

'Whaddya think?'

I nodded and tossed the body brush into the grooming kit. 'Sounds great.'

I had the feeling I was going to wind up caught in my own sticky web. Again.

'Girls!' called a voice. We looked up. Mrs McMurray was standing by the stable door. 'Drop past my office, will you? I've got a special job for you.'

'Yes, Mrs McMurray,' I said. I untied Bartok and emptied into his feeding trough a carefully measured serve of chaff and pony pellets. 'You ready, Preezy-Boo?'

Pree laughed and tugged at my ponytail. 'Ready.'

★ ★ ★

'Come in, Ash, Pree,' Mrs McMurray called from behind her office door.

We squeezed through the door, giggling.

A skinny girl with red hair and a pale face was standing beside Mrs McMurray. She smiled sweetly and waved. 'Hi, Ash!'

I was so shocked I felt as though my heart might stop.

'You know each other?' Mrs McMurray said.

'Oh, yes, Mrs McMurray,' Carly said. I wanted to throw up. 'We're friends from Riding Club. And we're in the same class at school.'

'Terrific!' Mrs McMurray said. 'I was going to ask both girls to show you around, but since you and Ash know each other so well, I'm sure Ash would love to do that herself, wouldn't you, lovey?'

I had a quick think. There were plenty of things I'd rather do than show Carly around. Like being branded. But I twisted my numb face into what I hoped was some kind of smile and jerked my head up and down. Carly grinned. I hated her so much. How could she do this to me?

'Then it's settled,' Mrs McMurray said, triumphant. 'Ash, love, give Carly the tour and explain the routine. Ooh, I have to tell everyone. There'll be an invitational riding competition here in two weeks' time — a chance for the whole district to see how fantastic Shady Trails is. Isn't that wonderful?'

Pree nudged me. 'Cool!'

I nodded, shell-shocked.

Mrs McMurray dismissed us and I pushed my way through the door. I had to check on Bartok and turn him out. Then there was Calypso, my favourite Ranch horse to catch, groom and tack up. But of course, what I really wanted to do was hide from Carly.

'Ashleigh!' called a voice. 'Aren't you supposed to show me around?'

I stopped dead in my boots. Pree moved past me, giving me a wink. Trust Carly. She sidled up to me, grinning like the pony who had the oats, the maize and the barrel of apples as well.

'What're you doing here, Carly?' I hissed.

'What does it look like? Working, just like you.' Carly brushed proudly at her brand-new Shady Trails jumper. 'Doesn't it look good on me? So new and clean.'

I looked down at my own jumper, which had looked as good as Carly's a few weeks ago. Now it was stained with horse and decorated with chaff husks, straw and what looked like a long black Bartok tail hair. Just the way I liked it.

I raised my chin. 'You're nothing like me. Why don't you take that off and get lost. We don't want people like you here.'

'Temper, temper, Spiller,' Carly sang. 'You'd better be nice to me or I might just have to go and bat my eyelashes at the old cheese and tell her how mean you've been to me. Might even manage to squeeze out a tear or two.'

I sucked in my breath. 'You are so—'

'How's it going, girls?' Mrs McMurray said, appearing suddenly at my side. 'Carly's so what?'

I opened and closed my mouth a few times. 'She's so, so ...'

Mrs McMurray watched me, perplexed.

'She's so welcome to Shady Trails.' I was amazed at my ability to say these words without choking on them.

Mrs McMurray smiled. 'That's the way, lovey.'

'Good on you, Spill—, ah, Ashleigh,' Carly said.

Mrs McMurray turned and walked back towards her office.

Carly wheezed, shaking with laughter. 'Nice one, Spiller. That was almost worth having to spend every future Saturday in your company.'

'Wish I could say the same for you,' I muttered.

My day didn't improve much after that (with the exception of Carly being put on muck-out duty for swearing in the holding yard). I rode home feeling flat; my world had been drained of colour and sound.

There was plenty of sound when I got home though.

'Ashleigh Louise!' My mother was shrieking. 'Ashleigh Louise Miller!'

I rode Honey into the corral and slid down to the ground, shuddering at the sound of my full name. When all three names are spoken in the same breath, I know I'm in gargantuan trouble.

'Get over here this instant and see what your toy horse has done!'

'Coming!' I moaned, untacking Honey. I rubbed her down quickly with a cloth nappy.

'Now!' Mum hollered.

I patted Honey's neck. 'Back in a minute, girl.'

I found Mum at the clothesline, so angry her fists were in bunches. She was glaring at Jason's clothes, which were strewn all about the lawn and covered with mud.

'What happened?' I said. 'Why'd you throw the baby's clothes in the dirt?'

Mum's face turned red. 'I did not throw the baby's clothes in the dirt, Miss. I found your pony pulling them down from the line, tossing them about and trampling on them.'

I laughed. 'No way.'

Mum's face turned even redder. 'Yes, way.'

I stopped laughing. It must be true. 'Where is he? Where's Toffee? How'd he get out of the paddock?'

Mum pointed to a bush and grunted. I sneaked over. Toffee was hiding under the bush, happily chewing on a pair of Jason's blue coveralls.

I snatched them. 'What're you doing?'

Toffee pulled back hard on the suit.

'You crazy horse,' I said. 'Give 'em here!'

I tugged harder. Toffee tugged back. I tugged some more. He tugged so hard I lost my balance and landed face-first in the bush. Then he wriggled out and took off across the lawn with Jason's suit still in his mouth.

I stood up, my mouth hanging open. 'That's the weirdest thing I've ever seen.'

'You're not wrong,' Mum muttered. 'Now help me clean up this mess.'

'But, Mum!' I whined. I was tired and hungry and all I wanted to do was watch TV and eat biscuits. 'It's getting dark.'

'Your horse did it, you clean it up. End of story.'

How could I argue with that?

I gathered all the clothes and put them in the washing machine, then set off after Toffee. I grabbed Honey's bag of carrots from the barn fridge, called to him and opened the paddock gate.

He appeared in front of me, a sleeve from the suit hanging from his mouth.

I offered him half a carrot. 'Isn't this better than a coverall?'

Toffee took a step towards me, his nostrils flaring again and again. He stretched out his neck and I held the carrot closer. My plan was to tempt him back into the paddock and let him eat the carrot there. He would learn that if he did the right thing he would be rewarded. Suddenly he lunged at me, grabbing the whole bag of carrots from my other hand and tearing away through the gate and across the paddock with the bag dangling from his mouth. I looked from him to the half carrot in my hand and shook my head. He was some horse, and I was in trouble.

Seventeen

Under the Hammer

'This is so wrong.'

I squeezed Becky's hand and stared at the round yard where Cassata was being led in circles. A number was pinned to her headstall. I couldn't believe we were so close to her at last. But it wasn't over yet. It was a long way from over.

'Have you got the money, Dad?' Becky said for the fifteenth time since we'd sat down in the grandstand.

'Yes, just try to relax!' Gary said, biting hard on his thumbnail.

Becky rocked back and forth. 'This is so awful, it's so terrible. Why can't we just go and take her back?'

214

'We've been through this,' Gary sighed. 'The dealer bought her, Becky. She's his until the hammer falls. Then she'll be ours again.'

The auctioneer launched into his garbled call and it had begun. Gary made the opening bid of two hundred dollars. Other people bid, raising what looked like ping-pong bats into the air. The price kept rising. Soon Cassata was worth one thousand eight hundred dollars. I squirmed, wanting to close my eyes, but at the same time not able to look away. Our girl. Our poor, poor girl. How frightened she must have been. To have been taken from her paddock, from the people who loved her and shunted from saleyard to saleyard. I focussed my mind on the empty float outside, and how Cassata would be back inside it soon and we'd be taking her home.

Becky's nails dug into my palm.

'It's going up,' she gasped. 'It keeps going up.'

'How much has your dad got?' I said.

Becky swallowed. 'Only three thousand. And that's with your Horse Cents money.'

The bidding didn't slow down for a moment. It seemed everybody wanted the sweet-faced Appaloosa mare and they were prepared to pay anything for her. The price rose and rose. Two thousand, two two, two three. I felt ill.

A bidder dropped out.

'Thank goodness!' Becky moaned.

'Do I hear two four?' cried the auctioneer.

Gary raised his paddle.

'Two five?'

A stiff-looking man with silver hair on the other side of the round yard raised his bat. He was with a girl who looked to be a little older than Becky and me, wearing dark purple joddies and wrapped in a matching purple jacket with something written across the back.

The bidding went on and on until Gary made his top bid of three thousand dollars. Becky crossed her fingers.

'Please, please,' she whispered.

'Do I hear three one?'

'Keep your ping-pong bat down, buddy,' I hissed. 'Keep it down.'

The silver-haired man's arm waved as he raised his paddle. My heart fell.

'Oh, no!' Becky cried. 'Dad, do we have any more money?'

My dad pulled out his wallet and opened it. He offered Gary three hundred dollars. 'Here, mate. Take this. It's all I have.'

Gary shook his head. 'No, it's not right.'

'Please, Dad!' Becky wailed.

Dad pushed the money into Gary's hands and he cleared his throat.

'Three three,' Gary called. I held my breath, watching as Purple Girl tugged on her dad's arm and stuck out her bottom lip.

The man raised his paddle again. 'Four thousand.'

'Crikey,' said Gary. He handed the money back to Dad.

'No!' Becky cried. 'No.'

'Four thousand going once,' cried the auctioneer. 'Twice.'

The crowd turned to look at Gary, waiting to see if he was going to make a move.

'Daddy, please, please,' Becky said. Tears were spilling down her face. 'I'll never ask you for anything ever again. Ever.'

Gary shook his head. He looked so old. So tired. 'Beck, I'm so sorry. I just can't.'

'Sold!' The hammer fell. Purple Girl jumped up and down, clapping her gloved hands. Silver Hair patted her head and smiled. He was the winner.

Becky slumped forward, sobbing. I cried with her. It was so unfair.

Cassata was led from the round yard while Silver Hair wrote in his chequebook. His daughter kissed his cheek.

Becky stood up suddenly and ran down the grandstand steps. I followed her, taking two steps at a time. She pushed her way past people until she was standing in front of Cassata for the first time in days.

Becky reached out her hand and Cassata rested her gentle brown eyes on her former mistress. Becky rubbed Cassata's nose and the mare took a step toward her. My heart ached so bad I could hardly breathe. Becky wrapped her arms around Cassata's neck.

'I love you, I love you so much.'

I covered my mouth and nose, trying to stop the tears.

Purple Girl wrenched on Cassata's lead rope. 'What do you think you're doing?'

Cassata's head was jerked away. Becky clung to her. 'She's my horse.'

'She's my horse,' said Purple Girl.

'I'll give you anything,' Becky cried. 'Anything. Just let me take her home.'

'I wouldn't want anything you could possibly offer. All I want is Spotty.'

'Spotty?' Becky frowned, confused. 'Who's that?'

'My horse, of course.' Purple Girl twisted her fingers around Cassata's headstall. 'Now, if you don't mind—'

'Her name's Cassata,' Becky said, grabbing the other side of the mare's headstall.

'It's Spotty. We bought her, I can call her whatever I want.'

'Spotty's a terrible name,' Becky cried. 'Please don't call her that. We've had her since she was a yearling. She's always been Cassata.'

'Not any more,' said Purple Girl. 'Daddy! Daddy!'

Silver Hair appeared at Purple Girl's side, tucking his chequebook into the inside pocket of his coat. 'What is it, Lauren?'

'Make these kids go away, Daddy. They're spoiling my whole day.'

'Just let me say goodbye to her,' Becky sobbed. She clung to Cassata's neck again. 'I'm sorry, girl. I'm so sorry!'

Gary tugged on Becky's arm. 'Time to go, Beck.'

'No, Dad, please!' Becky screamed. 'Please!'

Silver Hair muttered something to a man in a long white jacket and Cassata was led away. Lauren/Purple Girl trotted behind her. I could now read what was written on her jacket. *Landon Lodge*.

Gary pulled at Becky's arm but she thrashed about, crying out to Cassata. I was shocked. I'd never seen anyone so upset before. I didn't know what to do.

Gary picked Becky up and made a beeline for the exit. Dad grabbed my hand and squeezed it.

'Dad, what's happening?'

'She's hysterical,' Dad said. 'She needs to rest and have a drink. I'll go and have a look at her.' He jogged after Gary. I couldn't see him any more but I could hear Becky screaming. I looked around at the crowd. Everybody was watching me. I wiped at the tears on my face and ran after Silver Hair.

'Excuse me,' I called.

Silver Hair stopped and looked at me as though I were a pesky dog. 'What is it now? I hope you're not going to continue distressing my daughter.'

I shook my head. 'I just wanted your name and your number, if that's okay. Just so Becky can call and see how Cassata's doing.'

'I beg your pardon?'

'It's just with her lameness,' I lied. 'Becky always worries, although I can understand that. Especially after she foundered last year.'

'She foundered?' Silver Hair said. I was pleased to see that he looked a little ruffled. 'That's beside the point. I refuse to give out my personal details to a child. So go back to your father and leave me in peace.'

'Mr Landon,' said the man in the long white coat. 'Your horse is loaded.'

Mr Landon/Silver Hair took a final look at me and walked away.

'Please take care of her,' I called after him. 'She's a great horse.'

I watched him turn the corner and then followed him to the car park. Mr Landon climbed into the driver's seat of an expensive-looking four-wheel drive, which was hitched to a dark purple horse float. *Landon Lodge* was painted down the side in swirly silver writing. Underneath the writing was a phone number and a website address. I was furious. Landon wouldn't give me his number but was happy to advertise it to the whole world?

Landon and his float drove away taking Cassata to an unknown world. What would life be like for her at Landon Lodge? Would she be happy? Would Lauren Landon love her like Becky loved her? Would she kiss her and hug her and talk to her? Or would she be a plaything to use every once in a while for fun, but mostly ignored? As Cassata disappeared from our lives I sent one of my prayers up to the horse gods. Please let Cassata be okay, I begged. Please let her be happy. But mostly, let us get her back.

I made my way to the Chos' car, sick at the sight of the empty float and climbed into the back seat beside Becky. She was quiet now, but her breathing sounded strange, like she couldn't get enough air in. Gary started the engine and I picked up Becky's limp hand, squeezing it.

'S'okay, Becky,' I murmured. 'I know exactly where to find her. We'll get her back.'

I kept saying that, I know. But I had to convince Becky. Most of all, though, I had to convince myself.

Eighteen

Pony Tale

'There's something very very strange about that pony, Ashleigh Louise,' my mother grumbled three days later at breakfast.

'What do you mean?' I said, helping myself to two slices of bacon from the tray. I scooped up a fried egg with a lovely runny yolk and dumped it on my plate.

'Toffee broke into Mrs Adams's veggie patch last night and ate her entire corn crop,' she said, peering at me over the rim of her coffee cup. She rocked Jason's pram with her foot at the same time — 'multi-tasking' she calls it. 'So she chased him out with a rolled-up newspaper and he grabbed it and ripped it to shreds.'

'Mrs Adams across the road?' I mumbled through a mouthful of bacon and egg. 'The one who—'

'Threatened to call the police when you rode Honey across her front lawn?' Mum raised her eyebrows and offered me the toast rack. 'The very one.'

I swallowed, taking a slice of toast. A chunk of half-chewed bacon lodged in my throat. 'Was there much mess?' I gasped, reaching for my glass of milk.

Mum smiled, one of those horrid tight smiles that aren't smiles at all. They're more like fury-gauges. 'I'll say this much — the question is not, where did the newspaper go, but where didn't it go?'

'Do I need to clean it up?'

Mum laughed. 'Oh no, it's already been done. You see Mrs Adams, dear old thing, told me that if I didn't remove every scrap of sodden newspaper from her begonias and pay to have her corn replanted she'd call the council and have Toffee impounded.'

I wiped at my mouth with a paper serviette, not as hungry as I'd been in the seconds before the conversation had begun. I was befuddled. What was Toffee's problem?

'I'm working on it, okay, Mum?' I said, putting on my cutest, sweetest, please-don't-ground-me-until-I'm-eligible-to-vote face.

Mum wedged Jason's bottle back into his mouth. 'Work harder.'

Jason laughed. Only three months old and already ganging up on me!

'Can I take Jason outside?' I said, changing the subject.

Mum finished her coffee and nodded. 'Why don't you take him for a walk around the paddock and find the hole that your maniac pony is escaping through?'

I scraped my plate into the bin and stacked it in the sink, then drained my milk glass and balanced it on the plate. I wiped my mouth with the back of my hand.

'Disgusting,' Mum said.

'Thank you.' I grinned, tucking Jason's blanket around him until he was doing a pretty good impression of a caterpillar, and pulling his fluffy blue bear-ears hat down over his head. I pulled down the hood of his pram and hooked a pull toy on the rim. It was time for some intensive brother-sister bonding — and Jason's first horsemastership class.

* * *

'Never be nervous when meeting a pony for the first time,' I told Jason. I'd found Toffee nipping at Honey's heels in the paddock, caught him and tied him to the fence post in the corral. Jason was parked just outside. 'If you're nervous, the pony will be nervous.'

Jason gnawed on his fingers, watching me.

'Always speak quietly to ponies, Jason,' I said. 'In fact, always speak to ponies. That way they know where you are. They're less likely to get a fright and kick you.'

Jason yawned. His mouth was full of toothless gum.

'It's a good idea to offer a titbit to a pony, Jason. Just like this.' I offered a slice of carrot to Toffee holding my hand out flat, making sure my thumb was out of the way. Toffee sniffed the carrot, then snatched it, chewing happily. He leaned forward, searching for more, then, after not finding anything, nipped me right on the butt.

'Hey!' I yelled. 'That hurt, you monster!'

Toffee tossed his head, something that strongly resembled a huge grin spreading across his horsy face.

I grabbed hold of the seat of my joddies, rubbing hard. Jason laughed. Typical brother!

'I like you much better when you laugh than when you scream,' I said. 'It's okay if you scream when Flea's trying to sleep though. You have my blessing.'

'What's going on here?'

I peered over the corral, still rubbing my backside. Becky was mounted on Charlie in the driveway. She looked pale, but much better than she had when I'd last seen her.

'How's it going?' I said.

Becky shrugged, threw her leg over Charlie's shoulder and slid to the ground in the same way I do. I'd never seen her dismount that way before.

'We've tried everything,' she said. 'We looked up that website you said and Dad called the Landons.'

'Who are they, anyway?'

Becky opened the corral gate and led Charlie inside. 'Landon's a horse breeder. Racehorses.'

'Wow.' I untied Toffee and led him to the paddock gate, opening it and unbuckling his headstall. He cantered away, straight to a corner of the paddock. Toffee ducked down and wriggled. He was definitely up to something.

'Dad offered the Landons what they paid for Cassata but they're not interested. Lauren's always wanted an Appaloosa. They said no amount of money will convince them to give her up.'

I stared up at the sky, wondering why the horse gods had stopped listening to me.

'Dad tried to explain that Cassata was stolen from us but they reckon we're lying and they bought her at a legit auction and that's that.' Becky climbed up onto the corral fence, sighing. I'd never seen her so down. I knew that no matter what I did or said it wouldn't be enough. The only thing that would fix Becky would be to have Cassata back.

'Ash, Ash!'

Becky turned around. I climbed up the fence, waving madly at the sight of Pree cantering down our street on Jasmine. She turned Jasmine into our driveway and cantered her down to the corral, looking over her shoulder as she rode.

'What's happening?' I said, jumping down from the fence and opening the corral gate for her.

Pree pointed down the driveway. 'That's happening!'

The Creepketeers — Carly, Flea and Ryan — had gathered on their horses at the top of the driveway. They were shouting, jeering and making shapes with their fingers that would have seen me sentenced to a hundred hours of household chore service.

'They're loony tunes!' Pree said, panting. 'They found me just outside town and started chasing me and Jazz. Good thing I know where Shady Creek Riding Club is.'

'Are you okay?' I said.

Pree laughed. 'I'm fine. It was fun!' She stood up in her stirrups. 'Get outa here, ya losers!' she shrieked.

I ran to Jason and covered his ears. 'Pree, I was just telling Jason not to shout in front of ponies.'

Pree slapped her hand over her mouth. 'Sorry.' She held her other hand out to Becky. 'By the way, I'm Pree.'

Becky shook her hand warmly. 'Becky.'

I beamed, relieved to see my two friends getting along.

'How long did it take you to get here?' Becky said, rubbing Charlie's forelock.

Pree looked at her watch. ''Bout an hour. Of course, it would've taken longer if Jazz and I hadn't been running for our lives.'

Becky nodded. 'The Creepketeers have serious issues.'

Pree grinned. 'Creepketeers? I love it!'

I wheeled Jason inside for his nap while Pree and Becky got to know one another. By the time I came back to the corral, Becky had told Pree her version of the Cassata story.

'Doesn't sound like she needs saving,' said Pree.

'What?' Becky gasped. I had the sudden feeling that the meeting of friends honeymoon period had just ended.

'Landon Lodge is a nice place.' Pree took off her helmet and smoothed down her hair.

Becky stiffened. 'How would you know?'

Pree smiled. 'I've been there. Have you?'

Becky's face fell. 'No, but—'

'It's a number one horse breeding and training facility. It has everything. Cassata will be happy there. She'll have everything she needs.'

'But she won't have me.' Becky leaned her head against Charlie's shoulder.

Pree nudged my arm with hers. 'Tell her,' she said. 'Tell her Cassata'll be fine.'

I squirmed, torn once again between two friends. 'She's lucky the Landons got her instead of the ... well, you know.'

'Doggers?' Becky spat.

I looked at the ground, wishing something or someone would save me.

'I've got one for you,' Pree said suddenly. 'What's the most important part of a horse? The mane part!'

'And I've got one for you,' Becky said. 'Why did the horse cross the road? It was the chicken's day off!'

I smiled. Then I laughed and so did Pree and when I looked at Becky she was laughing too. I wrapped an arm around my friends' shoulders and pulled them into a hug. I had a strange feeling then that everything would be all right. No matter about the Creeps, Shady Trails and Riding Club, and poor lost Cassata — everything would be all right.

Nineteen

Once Ridden, Twice Shy

'There has to be a way to do this,' Pree said. She picked at her tub of fruit salad. 'Rats, no more apple.'

'We've tried begging.' I counted off on my fingers. 'We've borrowed money. We've gone to the police. Nobody's interested.'

I propped my chin in my hands at the lunch table. Most of the Ranchers had finished their lunch and were lounging around on squashy armchairs talking about horses.

'I've got it!' Pree jumped out of her seat. 'The Shady Trails Show!'

'What about it?'

'We can raise money. The Landons might not want to sell Cassata for what they paid, but they'd be crazy to say no to more. And we can get people aware of what's happened so that nobody else loses a horse this way.'

'I could sell ribbon browbands.'

'Huh?' Pree raised her eyebrows.

'I make 'em. I know — we could get a petition going! Get people to sign that they agree Cassata should be given back to the Chos.'

'Cool!' Pree said, offering her hand for a high-five.

'How about I start a petition?'

I looked up. 'Get lost, Carly.'

'Ooh, ooh,' Carly squeaked, jumping up and down and waving her hands. 'I know — I could get a petition going to ban Pinedork Ridge Riding Clubbers from being allowed to cross the Shady Creek border.'

'What's wrong with you, Carly?' I said. 'Isn't there some huge pile of horse poo out there with your name on it?'

'Or how about a petition showing that everyone

here agrees that Spiller and her mule sucked at the gymkhana and that Shady Trails needs real riders.'

I stared up at her, hating her more than ever.

'And another thing — why are you wasting your time trying to buy back that old nag? The Landons'll come to their senses eventually and when they do, they'll be dropping her off at the knackery themselves.'

Pree gasped and slapped her hand over her mouth.

I rubbed my forehead, wishing it all — wishing Carly — would go away.

I couldn't take it any more. I'd already quit Riding Club. Now I'd have to quit Shady Trails. How could I cope with Carly at school and at work? It was too much to ask of anybody. I pushed my chair back and stood up. I would find Mrs McMurray and tell her I was through at the Ranch.

Carly looked around the room, which had gone quiet. The Ranchers were all watching her. Carly beamed at them, pleased with herself.

Sam stood up. Azz stood behind her. They took a few steps closer to the table then stopped. Sam folded her arms, her eyes fixed on Carly. Azz fixed his eyes on Sam. Carly didn't look so pleased any more.

'Tell us all about how you were disqualified from Waratah Grove contention, Carly,' said Sam. 'What'd they get you on again?' Sam rubbed her chin thoughtfully. 'Was it cruelty to animals or dangerous riding?'

'Or having a big mouth?' Pree said, folding her arms like Sam.

Carly's face drained of colour. 'How do you—'

Sam smiled. 'Oh, I know everything. And I'll tell you another thing I know. I know the door's that way.'

Pree stood up, clapping her hands and whistling.

'And by the way,' Sam said, leaning in so close to Carly that she took a step back. 'Don't let me catch you speaking that way about a horse in front of me. Ever!'

Carly looked from one Ranch face to another then turned and ran for the door. I sighed, relieved.

Sam smiled. 'If she gives you two any more trouble just give me a hoy.'

'You can count on that!' I said.

'Let's get back out there!' Sam called to everyone. The Ranchers scrambled to their feet.

* ★ ★

By the time I got home that afternoon all I wanted to do was eat. But, as had so often happened since Jason had been born, there was no dinner. Instead of preparing me a delicious and nutritious evening meal my parents were poring over maps of Shady Creek, which they'd spread all over the table and were writing on a piece of crumpled paper.

'What's going on here?' I demanded. My head ached and my stomach growled.

'Never you mind,' Dad said.

'That you, Ash?' Mum said. She didn't even look up from her map, but pointed to something and tapped Dad on the shoulder. Dad smiled and wrote on the paper.

'No, it's the ghost of hot dinners past,' I grumbled, wrenching open the fridge door. 'Don't tell me. We're having cereal again, aren't we?'

'Hmm,' Dad said.

I took it as a 'yes, Ashleigh, we are having cold cereal instead of a nice cooked dinner and what's more you can fix it yourself' and made myself a bowl of cereal and cold milk with banana sliced over the top.

I sat at the table shovelling in spoon after spoon, glaring at my parents, wishing that the powers of telepathy I'd been trying so hard to perfect actually worked.

'We'll have to finalise the cost.'

'You're a plumber, you can work out the logistics.'

'I've just had enough of the nine to five.'

'This way you'll see more of the kids.'

They were up to something.

I finished my cereal and dumped the empty bowl in the sink. 'Thanks for dinner. It was delicious.'

'Huh?' Mum looked up at last. 'When did you come in?'

'What dinner?' Dad scratched his head with the tip of his pencil.

'Funny you should say that, Dad, coz it's the first thing I thought when I got home.' I returned the box of cereal to the third shelf and slammed the pantry door.

'Don't eat anything,' Mum said, going back to her map. 'We've ordered pizza.'

I clutched my forehead and collapsed on the kitchen floor. If they didn't starve me they'd drive me insane before my twelfth birthday.

Mum peered over the edge of the table at me. 'This should make you feel better.'

'What?' I groaned. Dessert. Maybe they'd organised some dessert for once.

'Toffee—'

I sat up. 'What? What'd he do this time?'

'Well,' Mum said slowly, like she was trying to figure out how best to break it to me. 'I've changed my mind about him. I no longer think he's pesky. I am now convinced he's completely nutty.'

I scrambled to my feet. 'What happened?'

'Why don't you go and see for yourself?' Dad said. He looked up at me and smiled.

I ran for the kitchen door, flung it open and tore down the steps and out into the backyard. Where was he? I heard a wild horsy shriek coming from the paddock and my heart stopped. My goodness. Was he hurt? Was that what my parents were trying to tell me?

I ran to the paddock and squeezed through the rails in the fence rather than waste the few seconds it would have taken to open the gate. I couldn't believe what I was seeing.

Toffee was galloping across the paddock with a half-deflated soccer ball in his mouth. He flicked his head and let it go, sending it soaring into the sky, then screeched to a halt, staring up at it, watching, waiting. It dropped and Toffee stamped. His eyes were fixed on the ball. He took off at a gallop again until his rump was just underneath it and, lashing out with his hind legs, kicked the ball. He spun around and chased the ball, snatching it up with his teeth then began the whole game again.

It came to me then, an idea so brilliantly amazing that I astonished myself. I had a surefire plan to get Cassata back and Toffee was going to help me do it.

Twenty

Horse Power

'So what's this big surprise you've got organised?' Becky said, checking Charlie's bridle.

'If I tell you it won't be a surprise, will it?' I smiled, triumphant. 'But I can promise you you've never seen anything like it.'

'How do you like Shady Trails, Becky?' Pree said. She settled into her saddle and swung her feet forward, making sure her stirrups were the right length. Jasmine tossed her head as if to say, 'Aren't you finished yet?'

'It's awesome,' Becky gasped. 'Totally awesome! I can't believe I stayed away for so long.'

I smiled then put my left foot into my stirrup, grabbed hold of the pommel and bounced into my saddle.

'Hey,' Becky said suddenly, 'I'm sorry about all that stuff.'

'All what stuff?'

'Before. When you started working here. I should never have told you to quit.' Becky mounted Charlie and gave me a sheepish look.

I shrugged. 'It's all forgotten, Beck. Just as long as we're best friends, nothing else matters.'

'You guys ready to ride?' Pree said. Jasmine certainly was. She danced on her forelegs and shook her head.

The Shady Trails Riding Ranch Show was about to start.

Honey and I were entered in the Open Rider 9 Years and Under 13 Years, the Ridden Galloway, Girl Rider 9 Years and Under 13 Years, classes in which we had to walk, trot and canter in the direction given to us by the announcer. We were also entering the Pony/Horse with the Longest Tail and Mount with the Prettiest Decorated Tail classes so we had our fingers and hooves crossed. Becky talked me into the Pair of Riders Under 13 Years class as well. By lunch I had won a blue ribbon for Honey's tail braid (thank you, Mrs Strickland!) and a red in the Open Rider (I lost to a kid from Pinebark Ridge) so I was pretty pleased with my haul. Becky had cruised in for a blue in the Girl Rider and Pree had scooped three blue ribbons on Jasmine winning Longest Mane, Longest Tail and Bareback Rider Under 13 Years.

'This food is great,' Becky said, taking a huge bite of her sausage, onion and tomato sauce roll. Azz had been busy behind the barbecue all morning. Becky swallowed and took a long drink of orange juice. 'Do you guys eat like this all the time?'

'Nuh,' Pree said. 'And it's a good thing, too. We'd wind up squishing our horses!'

I crammed the last bite of my sausage sandwich into my mouth and stood up, brushing crumbs from my lap. 'I gotta go.'

'Where?' Becky mumbled. She was chewing again.

'The surprise,' I said. 'Show's on in half an hour. Meet me in the holding yard.'

I dashed away, leaving my two friends staring after me.

I jogged through the crowds of riders, Ranchers, spectators and visitors to the stables. There was someone special waiting for me. And a bag. A bag that held a soccer ball and a folded piece of paper.

'Are you sure you wanna do this?' Becky said. Her eyes were wide.

'Good on you, Ash,' Pree said. 'I'll help out in the crowd.'

'Great,' I said, thrusting my riding helmet into her hands. 'Use this as a bucket. Get whatever you can.'

'Where'd you get that?' Becky said, pointing at the megaphone that I'd rested by my feet.

'Sam,' I said. 'She said she was too afraid to know why I wanted it.'

'Better get the show on the road, I suppose,' Pree said. 'Before the afternoon events get started.'

I nodded, nerves spinning so fast in my guts it felt like I'd eaten a bowl of bicarb for lunch.

Pree dashed from the holding yard and through the fence. I could hear her announcing that a big show was about to start and within minutes a crowd had gathered. I'd never been in this position before. I'd had to get up and accept ribbons, but I'd never had to say anything. I felt sick and afraid. What if I made a fool of myself? What if nobody cared about what I had to say? What if the star of the show went on strike? There were so many 'what ifs', each more horrible than the other.

I picked up the megaphone and cleared my throat. The crowd became quiet. They watched me, waiting.

'Ladies and gentlemen,' I said. More like I squeaked, I was that nervous. I unfolded the piece of paper I'd brought from home and began to read. 'Thank you for taking the time to see our show. We're here this afternoon to entertain you and also to inform you of a terrible situation.'

I cleared my throat again. It felt tight and sticky. I couldn't bear to look at the crowd. I wasn't sure if they were still there.

'A few weeks ago my best friend's horse was stolen. We tried everything we could to find her and bring her home but she was sold at auction. We need your help to raise awareness of horse theft and ask all of you here today to take measures to protect your horses. We also ask that you donate whatever you can to help us bring Cassata home. We love her and we miss her and we want her back.'

I handed the megaphone to Becky and dashed into the stables, leading Toffee out into the holding yard. I held up the soccer ball for the crowd to see and showed it to Toffee. His nostrils quivered and he tossed his head.

'Not yet, buddy boy,' I whispered.

I threw the ball up into the air a few times, then put it down on the ground and kicked it to Toffee. Toffee looked at me for a moment, looked at the ball, then turned his tail and walked away. I panicked. Had he forgotten how to play? Was he one of those 'never perform on request' types? The crowd was silent, still, watching.

Toffee stopped and looked over his shoulder at the ball. Then he arched his back and lashed out with his hind legs sending the ball flying into mid air. I ran for it and pounded it with my head back to Toffee who leapt into the air, catching it in his mouth and tearing around the round yard. The crowd cheered. I chased Toffee and he tossed the ball back over his head. I caught it and kicked it sending

Toffee after it in a mad scramble. A boy in the crowd asked if he could have a go and, after checking with his mum, I said he could. Then I had a thought.

'For five dollars,' I said.

The boy looked up at his mother, who reached into her bag pulling out her purse and her camera at the same time. Soon there was a queue. And after an hour we'd raised a hundred dollars. Once the last girl had kicked the ball to Toffee and posed with him for a photo I led him back to the stables and into Honey's stall, praising and thanking him. He'd done so well and been so good. And I knew that if she could, Cassata would thank him, too. I rubbed Toffee down and filled his water trough and haynet, then ran back to my friends. The day wasn't over — we had ribbons to win!

'This is for Cassata,' Becky murmured, rubbing a soft blue ribbon between her fingers.

I slipped my arm around Becky's shoulder. Pree patted her knee. We sat for a while not saying anything.

Mrs McMurray walked past, happier than I'd ever seen her.

'Girls,' she said, smiling. 'Having a good day?'

'Definitely,' I said. Pree and Becky agreed.

'You don't look so happy.' Mrs McMurray examined us all, her thoughtful blue eyes resting on each of us in turn. 'What could possibly wrong on such a wonderful day?'

'Well,' Becky began. She told the whole story of Cassata from start to finish with a little help from me and Pree.

'So that's what the miniature pony circus was all about today,' Mrs McMurray said.

'Yes, I'm sorry about that, but I just thought it'd be a great way to raise—'

'It's okay, Ash, love,' Mrs McMurray said, holding up her hands. 'I would've done the same if I were you. Well, maybe not the exact same. After all, I've never seen any horse do anything quite like what yours did today. Next time though, ask me first.'

My face burned, but Mrs McMurray smiled.

'You know, Reg Landon and I go back a long way. Would you like me to have a word—'

Becky jumped to her feet and grabbed Mrs McMurray's hands. 'Please, Mrs McMurray. Please, I'll do anything.'

'I can't make any promises, lovey,' Mrs McMurray said. 'How much did you raise today?'

'Five hundred and twenty-eight dollars,' Pree said at once.

'With the four thousand you already offered I'd say that's a fair price for a twelve-year-old mare.' Mrs McMurray smiled and walked away.

I nudged Becky. 'Everything'll be all right, Beck. It will.'

'It'll be better once you come back to Riding Club.'

I stared at the ground, avoiding Pree's eyes. 'I dunno, Beck.'

'How can I survive without you?'

'Why don't you join Pinebark Ridge with Ash?' Pree said, a huge smile on her face.

'Ash'd never do that,' Becky said, shaking her head. 'That's impossible.'

'She told me so herself, didn't you, Ash?'

I stared hard at my fingernails, wondering if I'd ever see them clean in my lifetime. I also wondered how on earth I was going to get around this one without hurting anybody. 'I, uh . . .'

'Ashleigh?' Becky said.

'Yes, Ashleigh?' Pree folded her arms.

'I did quit Shady Creek,' I began.

'Yes?' my friends said together.

'And I did say I'd join Pinebark Ridge.'

'Uh-huh,' said Becky, nodding.

'But, I'm so busy here at Shady Trails that I reckon I need a break from Riding Club for a while.'

'You'd be mad to join the Ridge anyway,' Pree said.

'What?' I thought she'd be upset.

'It took me an hour to ride to your place. You don't have a float. Why would you ride all the way out to the Ridge when you can go next door?'

'What are you saying?' I said, hopeful.

'Go back to Shady Creek Riding Club,' Pree said, her smile so wide and bright it put the sun to shame.

I stared at her, not sure what to say.

'Good, it's settled,' Becky said. She looked at her watch. 'Leaping Lipizzaners, I'm gonna be late!'

She scrambled to her feet, her long black plaits flying behind her as she disappeared into the crowd.

'Thanks for that,' I told Pree.

'No worries,' Pree said. 'I want you to be happy. And leaving Becky all alone with those Creepeleers wasn't going to make you happy.'

'Creepketeers,' I said. 'And no, it wasn't.'

I wrapped my arm around Pree's shoulder. 'Have I ever told you what a great friend you are?'

Pree shook her head. 'Nope, but now's a good time to start.'

'You're a great friend, Preezy-Boo.'

Pree giggled. 'So are you.'

We hauled each other to our feet.

'Hey, Ash, why did the horse go to the doctor? He had hay fever! Get it? Hay fever!'

'I get it, Pree,' I said, rolling my eyes.

'Why was the rodeo horse so rich? He had a lot of bucks.' Pree doubled over, laughing.

'You're mad,' I said, holding her up.

She nodded, gulping. 'Horse mad!'

'Totally horse mad.' I linked arms with my friend feeling like the luckiest girl on the planet.

Twenty-one

Lucky Horse

'This is Becky's place, here,' I said.

'I hope she's home,' Mrs McMurray said. She parked the Shady Trails Riding Ranch horse trailer on the street outside the Chos' place. It was early. So early in fact that I knew Becky would probably still be sitting at the table in her pyjamas.

'Well,' Mrs McMurray said. 'What do you reckon?'

Mrs McMurray opened the door and slid from the driver's seat to the road. I joined her and before long we'd lowered the ramp and led a sweet-faced mare out and up the Chos' front path.

'Want to do the honours, Ash?' Mrs McMurray said when we reached the front door.

'Next time,' I said. 'This is all thanks to you. You should do it.'

Mrs McMurray smiled, a smile so bright she could have given the sun a run for its money, and knocked hard on the Chos' front door.

'Ash?' Becky said. 'I saw you pull up. What—'

Becky's mouth dropped open. She stared at the mare, then burst through the door and threw her arms around her neck, tears running down her face.

'Cassata!' she cried. 'I can't believe it!'

Becky held her horse for a long time. Mrs McMurray and I said nothing. We just let her cry and kiss and shake her head.

'What's going on?' Rachael Cho appeared at the door and gasped. She looked so different. There was no make-up on her face and she was wearing a pair of riding boots. 'How? Who did this?'

'Mrs McMurray did everything,' I said.

Rachael looked from me to Mrs McMurray, her face pale with shock. 'Th-thank you. Thank you.'

Mrs McMurray smiled. 'You're quite welcome, love.'

'But how? I c-can't afford to pay for her. Not what those Landons were asking.'

'Landon owed me a favour or two. He was pretty reasonable. It didn't take too much convincing on my part.'

'I can't accept her.' Rachael sniffled.

'You have to,' Mrs McMurray said. 'I won't take no for an answer. But there is one condition.'

'What is it?' Rachael said, a single tear running down her face. 'I'll do it, whatever it is. I never knew how much Cassie meant to me until I, well. You know what I did. I was wrong.'

'It's a miracle,' Becky cried. 'Somebody call the newspapers!'

Rachael stared hard at the ground. Mrs McMurray took her hand.

'Sometimes we need to take a wrong turn to realise that we were on the right path to begin with.'

Rachael nodded, swallowing hard.

'Just one condition,' Mrs McMurray said again.

'Anything.' Rachael reached her hand out to her horse. Cassata touched her nose to Rachael's fingers.

'Come work for me. I need a trail leader and from what I hear they don't come much better than you, lovey.'

'Me?' Rachael pulled a face.

'You know what a hot rider you were, Rachael,' Becky mumbled through mouthfuls of Cassata's mane. 'Until you went sick in the head.'

'I wasn't bad,' Rachael admitted.

'Deal?' Mrs McMurray held out her hand.

Rachael shook on it. 'Deal.' She took a few steps closer to her horse and wrapped her arms around Cassata's neck, telling her how sorry she was and promising to never let her go again.

It was over. I was so relieved. To have Cassata back was incredible. To see her reunited with Becky was something I'll never forget. To hear Rachael say she was wrong was miraculous. In all, it was a pretty unreal morning.

Twenty-two

Gallop Inn

'Are you sure you have enough time for this ride?' I bit at my bottom lip the way I always do when I'm nervous.

'I always have time for horses,' Mrs McMurray said, settling into her deep stock saddle. 'Besides, we have lots of things to talk about, lovey.'

Mrs McMurray urged Clarence, her huge bay gelding, out of the holding yard gates and down one of the many trails the property had to offer.

'D'you like it here?' I said at last.

Mrs McMurray nodded. 'Very much. I'm relieved, you know.'

I was confused. 'Relieved. Why?'

Mrs McMurray smiled. 'Because I've finally achieved what I've always wanted to, lovey. I was scared, I can't deny it. But I did it. I built my Riding Ranch.'

'I'm glad you did,' I said, patting Honey's neck. She was being perfect and I had to reward her.

'And what about you, Ash, love?'

'Me?'

'And Linley. Have you had a think?'

I nodded. 'I have.'

'And?'

'I'm going to have a go. I'm going to apply for a scholarship.'

Mrs McMurray sighed. 'That's terrific!'

I grinned. It was wonderful. Linley was wonderful. I'd miss Mum and Dad and Jason. But to ride every day, to learn more, to be the person I knew I had to be — I was applying. There was nothing in the world I wanted more.

'Thank you,' I said.

Mrs McMurray frowned. 'What for?'

'For Linley. For telling me about it and all that,' I said. 'For believing I have a chance. Even if I don't get it I feel like I already did. Coz you believe I can. Do you know what I mean?'

She nodded, pulling Clarence up. The gelding stood still and quiet. Honey stood beside him and the horses touched noses.

'And Ash,' Mrs McMurray said, reaching into the pocket of her jacket, 'this is for you, lovey.'

She held out a small velvet bag. I took it.

'What is it?'

'Open it and see.'

I opened the bag, my fingers so cold and stiff they hardly worked at all. I tipped the contents of the bag into my open hand. It was a horse, a pendant of a horse made from glass. But not just any glass. This was glass like I'd never seen before. It was like opal — blue and gold and purple and green together and sparkling like a jewel. I loved it.

'It's amazing,' I said.

'Put it on.' Mrs McMurray watched me eagerly, pleased I liked her gift.

'But this is too good. What about your granddaughters? Shouldn't you give it to one of them?'

Mrs McMurray smiled. 'I could have. But I wanted to give it to you.'

'Really?' I was so honoured.

'Really. Now that reminds me, Ash, love. I'm going to need your help.'

I held tight to my pendant. 'Anything.'

'I had a phone call from my son a few days ago. He's travelling around Australia on business and asked if his girls can come to stay here with me at Shady Trails. I told him I'd love to have them. But I was hoping you'd help me with them.'

I swelled with pride. Of all the people Mrs McMurray could have asked, she was asking me. 'I'd love to!'

Mrs McMurray beamed. 'Now, put on your pendant, love. And when you're riding at Linley you can wear it and remember why it's you who deserves to be there.'

'I'm not there yet.'

'You will be. Now, put it on.'

My fingers weren't so stiff any more. I opened the clasp and secured the pendant around my neck, touching it at once.

'Gorgeous,' Mrs McMurray said, smiling.

'Thank you,' I said.

'You're welcome. Now, let's get these creatures home and ready for bed.'

We rode back down the trail together as the sun sank slowly before our eyes. I was sure it was a sign — the horse gods had heard me and answered my prayers. Everything was finally working out just right and I was happy.

'Well, what do you think?' Mum said when I got home that night. She gestured to the steaming pot of dinner on the table.

Dad was holding Jason, who squealed with delight when he saw me. I didn't know what I was more stoked to see — Jason or the beef stroganoff.

I sat down, my mouth watering. Mum piled rice on my plate then slopped a huge serving of stroganoff over the top. It smelled awesome. I took a bite. It tasted unreal.

'This isn't bad,' I said. 'Although the cereal is calling my name.'

'Don't worry,' Dad said. 'You can still have the cereal.'

I shook my head, my mouth full of food. 'Nooayyy.'

Dad frowned. 'Huh?'

'That could have been "no way",' said Mum.

I nodded, chewing.

'Ash, we have some news,' Dad said. He gazed at Jason like he was the most perfect being that had ever breathed. Let's face it, he wasn't a horse, but he was pretty close to perfect. For a boy, anyway.

I swallowed. 'What?'

Their news had the habit of being earth-shaking. Moving house, new babies ... oh, no! It couldn't be.

I pointed at Jason, dread seeping into the pit of my stomach. 'Not again. Please don't tell me you're having another baby!'

Dad shook his head. 'Nope.'

'It's Toffee, isn't it? What's he done this time?'

'He's actually been almost horse-like today,' Mum said.

'Well, what then?' I couldn't handle this guessing game.

'I'm taking a year off work,' Dad said. 'It'll be so great to spend some time at home with you and Jason, and Mum of course.'

'Of course,' Mum said, stifling giggles.

'But what are we gonna do for money? Remember what things were like last year?'

I almost couldn't bear to remember. Last year when Mum was out of work and we couldn't afford to get the vet out for Honey. It was too awful.

'I have some savings,' Dad said. 'And there'll be money coming in in other ways.'

'Are you going back to work?' I fixed my eyes on Mum, my dinner forgotten.

Mum shook her head. 'Not yet. I will eventually, but Jason could be the last Miller baby. I want to enjoy him as long as I can.'

'Should I leave school? Work at Shady Trails full time?' I fluttered my eyelashes and put on my very best smile.

'No!' both my parents cried at once.

'We've decided to open up a B and B,' Mum said, anxiously, like she was trying to put any ideas I had about leaving school to bed until I was at least thirty-five.

'A what?'

'A bed and breakfast,' Dad explained, bouncing Jason on his lap. 'A place like a hotel, where people stay overnight, have breakfast and carry on with their travels.'

'A hotel? Us? Here in Shady Creek?' I was amazed. My eyes were so wide I wasn't sure I'd ever be able to close them again.

'Us,' said Mum.

'We've been thinking about names,' Dad said. Jason gnawed on his fingers and smiled. 'Any ideas?'

'Gallop Inn,' I said at once. 'Canter Inn? Piaffe Inn?'

'We'll see,' Mum said, laughing.

'I have some news as well,' I said, staring hard at my plate. I wanted to tell them but at the same time I didn't.

Dad's face fell. 'Don't tell me you're opening up a B and B as well. Your mum and I will be ruined.'

I threw my paper serviette at him. 'Dad!'

He reached across the table and tousled my hair. This time I didn't mind a bit.

'I've decided to go for a scholarship. At Linley Heights.'

I looked up slowly, bracing myself for the howls of loving protest.

'That's tops, Ash. Top stuff,' Dad beamed.

'Huh?' I was confused. What about the 'please don't leave us all alone dearest only daughter' speech? Had I missed something?

Mum filled her glass with water. 'We're behind you, Ash. Two hundred per cent of the way. Happy?'

I nodded, raising my glass of apple juice. 'To Gallop Inn.'

Mum raised hers. 'To Shady Creek.'

'To scholarships at Linley Heights!'

Dad raised Jason. Jason giggled and kicked his chunky legs. 'To us!'

I put down my glass and held out my hands, scooping Jason from Dad's arms and holding him close. I closed my eyes and rested my forehead against my brother's, feeling the warmth of his soft baby skin. So much had happened but I knew that so much more lay just around the corner. I was happy and life was good.

Glossary

bash to 'give it a bash' means to give something a try

bicarb abbreviation for sodium bicarbonate, or baking soda

brumbies Australian wild or feral horses

doona comforter or quilt

Eskies coolers or ice chests

farrier someone who specializes in fitting horseshoes

footy a game similar to rugby, but unique to Australia

grotty gross

gymkhana an equestrian event, usually for young people, that involves timed games for riders on horses

hack to 'go for a hack' means to go for a walk or a slow canter on a horse

hoy a yell or a shout

joddies abbreviation for jodhpurs

joggers running shoes

kindy abbreviation for kindergarten

knackery a facility where horses are made into dog food or glue

muck-out barrow a wheelbarrow used while cleaning out a horse's stable

nappy diaper

nong idiot

paddock a small field or plot of land

pram a baby's stroller

scrummy abbreviation for scrumptious

telly abbreviation for television

tomato sauce ketchup

ute a pickup truck; abbreviation for utility vehicle

Acknowledgements

I would like to thank my publisher at HarperCollins, Lisa Berryman, and my editor, Lydia Papandrea, for their guidance and support. Thank you to my gorgeous kids, to my wonderful family and to my amazing lifelong friends. Thank you to Georgia for teaching me so much about horses. And thank you to Seb, my soul mate, for your love and friendship.

Photo by Dyan Hallworth

KATHY HELIDONIOTIS lives in Sydney and divides her time between writing stories, reading good books, teaching and looking after her three gorgeous children. Kathy has had eleven children's books published so far. *Horse Mad Heroes* is the fourth book in the popular Horse Mad series. Watch out for Book 5, *Horse Mad Western*, coming soon.

Visit Kathy at her website:
www.kathyhelidoniotis.com

Also by Kathy Helidoniotis

Totally Horse Mad

ISBN 978-1-55285-952-0

When her two best friends don't get along, Ashleigh's summer doesn't go quite to plan...

Horse Mad Summer

ISBN 978-1-55285-953-7

Standards are high at the riding academy. Can Ashleigh and Honey make the grade?

Horse Mad Academy

ISBN 978-1-55285-959-9